THE BOBBSEY TWINS'
FOREST ADVENTURE

THE BOBBSEY TWINS BOOKS
By Laura Lee Hope

"The boys trained the chemical hose onto the fire

The boys trained the chemical hose onto the fire

The Bobbsey Twins' Forest Adventure

By

LAURA LEE HOPE

GROSSET & DUNLAP

Publishers   *New York*

CONTENTS

THE BOBBSEY TWINS' FOREST ADVENTURE

Flossie quickly removed the loop from Waggo's leg

CHAPTER I

A FARAWAY MYSTERY

"STAND back!" Bert Bobbsey ordered. "A few more whacks and this tree will topple." He swung his hatchet again and the small maple shuddered.

"It will fall any second now," Nan observed excitedly. "Move away, Freddie and Flossie!"

Dark-haired Bert and Nan were twelve-year-old twins. Freddie and Flossie, twins also, were six and blond. Their blue eyes danced with glee as they watched Bert chop the tree beside the garage in their back yard.

The afternoon sun, this early June day, glinted off the hatchet as it bit deep into the trunk again. This time the tree started falling slowly toward Flossie.

"*Timber!*" Freddie cried.

"Look out, Flossie!" Nan shrieked and grabbed the little girl away just in time.

Crack! The tree hit the ground beside them.

1

"Oo, look what happened!" Flossie wailed, pointing at the ground. "It's broken! My badminton racket's broken!"

Bert and Nan pulled the fallen tree aside. Flossie was right. The maple's top branches had snapped the strings of the racket.

"You shouldn't have left it on the grass," Freddie remarked.

"We'll take it to the toy repair shop," Bert said. "Anyway," he added jokingly, "it's easier to repair this racket than Flossie's head."

At that moment a car pulled into the driveway and a tall, athletic-looking man stepped out.

"Dad, we did the job you wanted!" Bert called out to him.

Flossie ran to her father, who picked the little twin up in his arms and kissed her. "How's my Fat Fairy?" he said, as he put her down.

This was Mr. Bobbsey's pet expression for Flossie. He often called chubby Freddie his Fat Fireman, because Freddie had wanted to be a fireman ever since he had begun to play with toy fire engines.

Now Mr. Bobbsey walked over to the spot where the maple had stood. "Nice job, Bert," he commented. "Thank you. Too bad that storm last night split the tree."

"I hated to see it go," Nan said wistfully.

"Waggo will miss lying in its shade on hot days."

At the mention of his name, a frisky fox terrier bounded around the side of the Bobbseys' spacious home and raced up to Bert. Then the terrier stopped short, cocked his head, and looked at the fallen tree. A sad expression did seem to come into his brown eyes.

"We had to cut it down, Waggo," Flossie told him soothingly.

Mr. Bobbsey chuckled. "Don't worry, Waggo," he said. "We'll plant a new tree."

"Right now?" Freddie asked.

"Immediately," his father replied, smiling. "Hop into the car, all of you, and we'll get another tree. Come on, Waggo, you too!"

"Great!" exclaimed Freddie.

As they drove off, Nan remarked, "I hope we can find another maple tree as pretty as our other one."

"I'm sure we will," Mr. Bobbsey said.

In a few minutes they reached the nursery. The owner took them to a grove filled with slender young maple trees standing about six feet tall. Bert and Nan selected a sturdy-looking one, and the nurseryman dug it up.

The twins watched, fascinated, as the man encased the ball of earth around the roots with burlap. Waggo sniffed the covering.

"See, he's happy now!" cried Flossie.

After Mr. Bobbsey had paid for the tree, he and Bert carried it to their car and laid the maple in the rear compartment.

"Are my young lumbermen all set to plant their maple tree?" Mr. Bobbsey asked as he reached their back yard.

"Okay, Daddy, let's dig!" Freddie said gleefully. "We're a lumber family."

Mr. Bobbsey was a lumberman but not one who cut down forest trees. He owned and managed a lumberyard in Lakeport, where the Bobbseys lived, on the shore of Lake Metoka.

Freddie and Flossie ran to get a spade out of the garage. Bert and Nan, meanwhile, placed the new tree near the spot where the other had stood. Each of the twins took turns digging the hole.

"There, I guess that's deep enough, Bert," Mr. Bobbsey remarked finally.

Just then a pleasant voice said, "What a nice surprise!" The children turned to see their mother approaching. Mrs. Bobbsey was a slender woman with a pretty, smiling face.

Bert and his father lifted the tree gently into the hole. Nan and Flossie poured in water, then Freddie started to shovel the mound of earth back around it.

"There, now we have a brand-new tree!" Nan

said proudly, glancing at her father. Then she noticed a faraway look in his eyes. "What's the matter, Dad?"

"This tree," Mr. Bobbsey said, "reminds me of a mystery I have to solve."

"A mystery?" the twins chorused eagerly, and Bert added, "Maybe we can help you solve it."

The Bobbsey twins were fond of solving mysteries. They had had many wonderful times finding clues to baffling riddles. Their latest detective work had taken place at Pilgrim Rock. Now they all were thrilled at the idea of another exciting adventure.

"Perhaps you could help me," Mr. Bobbsey replied, "but I'm afraid this mystery is too far away."

"Where is it?" Nan asked.

"The problem is at Silver Creek, in the state of Washington," Mr. Bobbsey replied, casting a glance at his wife. "Shall I tell them about it, Mary?"

Mrs. Bobbsey nodded. "I think you should, Richard," she said. "The mystery really concerns all of us!"

The twins were intrigued by these words. Bert hurried to get two lawn chairs for his parents. When they were seated, the children sprawled on the grass, eager to hear about the Silver Creek mystery.

"It concerns my business," Mr. Bobbsey began. He explained that a man named Mr. Everett, an old friend of his, operated a gyppo logging outfit in which Mr. Bobbsey himself had an interest.

"Oh dear!" Flossie said in alarm. "Is Mr. Everett *gypping* you, Daddy?"

Her father chuckled. He explained that a "gyppo" was a sub-contractor who cut lumber for large lumber mills.

"But what about the mystery?" Bert urged.

Mr. Bobbsey explained that he had put up half the money for Mr. Everett's business, but now his partner was running into bad luck.

"Equipment has been stolen, among other things," said the twins' parent, looking grave. "We're losing money."

Nan's eyes widened. "Do you think someone is trying to ruin the business?" she asked.

"If he is, let's find him!" Freddie burst in importantly. "We'll all go there today!"

Nan smiled and explained to Freddie that Silver Creek was on the West Coast of the United States, a long distance from Lakeport.

"Besides," Mrs. Bobbsey added, bending to pat the curly-haired boy beside her, "it would cost a lot of money to take all of us out there."

Just then Waggo barked sharply and raced around the other side of the garage.

"Get away, Waggo!" came a boy's angry voice.

Bert leaped up and ran to see who was there. At this moment two boys jumped into view. One was Danny Rugg, a dark-haired boy of Bert's age, but heavier built and taller. The other was his pal, Jack Westley, who was usually Danny's companion in playing jokes on other people. Both boys had on cowboy chaps and sombreros. Danny twirled a lariat nonchalantly.

"Hello," said the twins, but not enthusiastically.

"We're playing cowboys and Indians," Danny said. He grinned. "Thought there might be something around here we could lasso."

Mr. Bobbsey spoke up. "If you want to play in our yard, boys, it's all right," he told them pleasantly. "But please don't do any damage. Mary," he said to Mrs. Bobbsey, "if you're ready we'll go downtown."

She turned to Bert and Nan. "Take care of Flossie and Freddie while I'm gone," she said.

After the car had left, Danny snickered. "Your father said we could play here. Jack, let's find something to lasso."

Bert and Nan watched the boys closely, because they had had many bad experiences with Danny and Jack, whose idea of fun was to annoy the younger twins.

"How about the new tree, Jack?" Danny suggested, a gleam of mischief in his eyes. "It's a swell target."

"No. Leave it alone," Bert said quickly. "You might hurt the bark."

"Ha, ha," Danny scoffed. "Speaking of bark, I'll lasso Waggo instead."

Before the twins could stop him, Danny twirled the lariat over his head, then threw it. The lariat dropped neatly over the terrier. Waggo leaped off the ground, but the rope caught his left hind leg. Danny smiled and yanked on the rope. The dog howled in fright.

"You're mean!" Nan cried, dashing toward Danny. "You let him go!"

"Try and make me!" Danny ran with the rope, pulling Waggo backwards on three legs.

"Stop!" Bert ordered. He lunged at Danny and pulled the rope out of his hand.

Flossie, near tears, bent down and quickly removed the loop from her pet's leg. Bert tossed the rope to Danny, who stepped forward and shoved the Bobbsey boy.

Bert shoved him back. Danny teetered, his feet becoming tangled in the rope. Jack Westley tried to catch him, but Danny fell on his back. His left hand went *squish* in the mud around the base of the new tree.

Freddie laughed loudly. "Serves you right, Danny."

"It isn't funny!" Jack blurted out loyally.

Danny, beet-red with anger, picked himself up and wiped the mud off his hands on the grass.

"I'll get even with you Bobbseys for this," he said. "Come on, Jack."

The two boys stalked out of the yard and down the street, muttering. Near the end of the block the twins noticed a thin, dark-haired man stop the bullies.

"I wonder who he is," said Nan. "The man's pointing toward us!"

Now Danny and Jack also pointed at the Bobbsey twins, and Jack held a hand to his face as if snickering.

"What can they be up to?" Nan wondered.

As the Bobbseys watched, the man quickly handed something to Danny and Jack. Their heads bobbed in agreement. Then together all three hurried off mysteriously!

CHAPTER II

A FLIP-FLOP FISH

BERT and Nan were worried. "I wish we'd had a better look at that man," Bert said, as the stranger walked along with Danny and Jack. "I'll bet they're up to something."

"Yes. We'll have to keep our eyes open," said Nan, then added, "I want to take Flossie's badminton racket to the repair shop. Come along?"

"Okay," her twin agreed. "We might want to play a game after supper."

As Bert went to pick up the racket, a small, dark-haired boy raced into the yard. He was six-year-old Teddy Blake, a freckle-nosed boy, one of Freddie's best friends.

"Hey, Freddie!" Teddy called. "Will you play with me? I have a swell idea for some fun."

"Sure," Freddie replied eagerly. "What do you want to do?"

Teddy grinned. "Come on down to my house," he suggested. "I'm putting up a tent."

"May I come too?" Flossie asked.

Teddy puckered his lips and frowned thoughtfully. "We're going to pretend we're hunters in a wild forest," Teddy explained. "I don't know if girls would like that. It's pretty dangerous—"

Hearing this, Nan smiled. "I think you'd better let the boys play alone, Flossie," she said. "How would you like to come to the toy-repair shop with Bert and me?"

"And look at the dolls there?" Flossie asked excitedly.

When Nan nodded yes, Flossie turned to the two little boys. "Go to your dangerous old forest if you like." She wrinkled her nose at her twin and Teddy, who raced off immediately.

"Dinah!" Nan called out.

In reply, a jolly, round face appeared at the kitchen window. "Yes, honey child. What is it?"

Dinah Johnson was a kindly colored woman who had helped Mrs. Bobbsey with the house-keeping for as long as the twins could remember. She and her husband Sam had an apartment on the third floor of the Bobbsey home. Sam drove a lumber truck for Mr. Bobbsey, and the couple were a beloved part of the family.

"Is it cookies you all want?" Dinah asked. " 'Cause if it is, I'm just puttin' a batch in the oven now. They'll be ready in half an hour."

Nan laughed. "We'll have some when we get back, Dinah," and she told the cook where they were going and where Freddie was.

"All right," Dinah said with a wave of her hand as the children hurried off.

"Let's look for Danny, Jack, and that stranger," Nan suggested, as they approached the business district of Lakeport.

"Yes," her twin replied. "It seems sort of mysterious, don't you think? If that man wanted to find out something about us, why didn't he come to our house?"

The Bobbseys looked right and left as they made their way toward the toy shop. But the stranger and the two boys were nowhere in sight. The toy-repair shop, located near the center of town, was a new one operated by a Chinese named Mr. Foo. Presently the three children reached it and went inside. As they closed the door, a delightful tinkle came from a string of sparkling colored glass strips which hung over the entrance.

The place was filled with all sorts of interesting objects, from Chinese box kites to glass tanks containing various kinds of tropical fish. On the shelves along the walls stood dolls, old and new, as well as many toys and games.

At the rear of the store was a counter. Back of it stood Mr. Foo, smiling broadly behind horn-rimmed eyeglasses.

"Hello, my young friends," he said with a little bow. "What can I do for you today?"

Bert held up the broken badminton racket. "Can you please restring this while we wait?" he asked.

Mr. Foo took the racket, turned it over, then looked up. "Yes, I can do it, but not this minute. I can have it ready for you in an hour."

"That'll be fine," Bert replied.

"You are welcome to look around the shop if you'd like," Mr. Foo said cordially.

Nan smiled. "Thank you. We will."

"Isn't everything bee-yoo-ti-ful?" Flossie asked, her large blue eyes blinking as she tried to take in all the items at once.

"There is an old Chinese proverb," said Mr. Foo, "that everything in life has beauty if you look for it, little girl." Smiling, he disappeared into a small room at the back of the store.

The two sisters turned their attention immediately to the dolls. Nan had a collection of them from many lands. She always looked forward to receiving new ones at Christmas.

"These modern dolls are cute," Nan said, "but I think I like the old-fashioned ones better, don't you, Flossie?"

Flossie looked at the shelf of antique dolls with china faces to which Nan was pointing.

"They look like pictures of our great-grandmother when she was young, don't they?" Flossie said, as she admired the period costumes the dolls wore.

"Yes, and see how pink and white the ladies' faces are," Nan pointed out. She laughed. "In olden times ladies never let themselves get a suntan!"

Nan longed to buy one of the antique dolls, but the price tags said fifty dollars. "I'd have to save my allowance for years to have one of those dolls," she told herself.

Bert, meanwhile, had looked first at a glass case containing Chinese puzzles. Now he was gazing at the tankful of tropical fish whose long tails swished slowly in the greenish water.

"Look at this beauty," Bert called out. "Here's an Angel fish."

Flossie skipped over to her brother. "I just love seafood," she said.

Bert chuckled. "These aren't to *eat!*" He put his arm around Flossie's waist and lifted her up for a better view into the high fish tank. "This is sea *life.*"

Flossie's chubby fingers grasped the edge of the tank, and without thinking she pulled it toward her.

"Don't do that!" Bert cried, but his warning came too late.

Water sloshed over the side of the tank, and with it came four rainbow-colored fish!

Luckily the tank did not overturn, and Bert quickly pushed it back to a safer position.

"Oo, the poor little fish!" Flossie cried, forgetting that she was all wet and that seaweed was dangling from her sunsuit.

Nan and Bert tried to pick up the fish, but they were so slippery and flopped around so violently that the twins could not hold them.

"Oh, they'll die out of the water!" Flossie wailed.

Hearing the commotion, Mr. Foo hastily came from his workshop. He grasped a small net hanging from the side of one of the tanks. With this he scooped up three fish which lay together and returned them to the tank.

"I'm so sorry," Flossie told the man. "It was all my fault."

"It is all right," Mr. Foo reassured her. "The fish were not injured. Do not worry."

Bert scanned the wet floor. "I'm sure I saw four fish slip out," he told the shop owner.

"I did, too," Nan spoke up. "Where could the other one have gone?"

Suddenly Flossie gave a little scream as she looked down at the front of her bright yellow sunsuit. "Here it is! In my pocket!" she cried.

She showed the others the tiny fish which was flopping feebly inside the pocket. Smiling, Mr. Foo picked it up gently, and a moment later the fish was swimming around with its mates.

Then the toy-repair man got a couple of cloths. Nan tried to dry Flossie's sunsuit.

Mr. Foo, meanwhile, wiped up the spilled water.

Grinning, he exclaimed, "Anyhow, I'm glad you found the missing fish before it was too late."

Bert said, "We'd better go outside and play while we're waiting for the badminton racket."

Nan agreed. The three children went to a near-by park, where they enjoyed the swings and slides for an hour. Then they returned to the repair shop.

"Your racket is ready," Mr. Foo said, as they entered.

Bert thanked him, paid for the job, and the children left the store happily.

On the way home, Nan remarked that they had picked up two mysteries in one day. "I wish we could find out about the man who was pointing at us. And then there's Dad's problem out West."

"He's sure worried about it," her brother remarked. "I wish we could help him."

"I know how," said Flossie. "By playing long-distance detectives. Just like they have long-distance telephones."

Nan laughingly said she wished that were possible. "If you figure it out, honey, we'll do it!"

As they walked up their street, Flossie was

deep in thought, remembering the beautiful antique dolls at the toy-repair shop. How she wished she could buy one for Nan on her next birthday! All at once she realized that they were nearly home.

"Oh, there's Dinah," Flossie said, running on ahead. "I'm going to get a cookie!"

The colored woman was standing on the Bobbseys' front porch, calling Freddie. "Have you seen him?" she asked as the three children approached.

"No, we haven't," Nan said. "Isn't he at Teddy's?"

Dinah appeared agitated. She said that Mrs. Blake had phoned to ask if Dinah knew where the boys were.

"I just can't imagine where they went," Dinah said, wringing her hands nervously.

"We'll find him," Bert offered.

Just then Teddy Blake raced into the Bobbsey yard. His face was pale, and tears were streaming down his cheeks.

"Mercy!" Dinah exclaimed. "Has something happened to Freddie?"

Teddy sputtered, out of breath, "Danny and Jack have caught Freddie and won't let him go!"

CHAPTER III

AN EXCITING CHASE

AS TEDDY BLAKE made his announcement Flossie began to cry. "Oh, they'll hurt Freddie! Danny and Jack are so mean!"

Bert asked where the boys were holding his small brother.

"In a vacant lot near Danny's house," the little boy answered.

"We'll go get him right away," Bert said determinedly. "Here, Waggo! Here, Snap! Come help us find Freddie."

Waggo came running from behind the house. Following him was Snap, the Bobbseys' other dog. Snap was larger than Waggo and had a shaggy white coat. He had been a circus dog before coming to live with the Bobbseys.

Flossie wanted to go, but Bert said he thought Freddie might have been moved and the trip might be a long one. So Flossie agreed to stay with Dinah but said, "Hurry and bring Freddie back!"

Bert and Nan hurried off with Teddy, who continued his story. "Freddie and I were playing in my tent," he said, "when Danny and Jack captured us. They lassoed us and took us to a lot full of high weeds."

"What happened then?" Bert asked, his fists clenched in anger.

"They didn't pay much attention to me," Teddy continued, "but they asked Freddie all about your father's trip to some place called Silver Creek."

Nan and Bert looked at each other. So the two mean boys had been eavesdropping at the Bobbsey home!

"But why would they want to know about Silver Creek?" Nan asked.

Bert snapped his fingers. "Say! I'll bet I know. Remember that mysterious man who talked to Danny and Jack? Maybe he asked them to find out!"

"But they didn't," said Teddy. "Freddie wouldn't answer any of their questions, so Danny said he'd have to stay there until he did. But they let me go."

"We'll fix them!" Bert said grimly.

As they approached the weed-filled lot, Teddy stopped and put a finger to his lips.

"Sssh!" he warned. "Danny and Jack may still be in there."

"Then we'll surround them," Bert ordered.

At his direction, Nan took Waggo and, bending low, crept to the other side of the lot. Bert and Snap stood guard on the opposite side while Teddy walked boldly to the place where he had been held prisoner.

Teddy walked through the weeds directly to the hiding place. Bert could barely see the top of the boy's head as he pushed through.

Then Teddy's voice came clearly. "Bert! Nan! Nobody's here. They've gone!"

The twins rushed to the little boy's side. The weeds and grass had been matted down where Freddie and Teddy had been held captives. But the only further evidence that anybody had been there were two short pieces of rope which Nan picked up.

"That's what they tied me up with," Teddy explained.

"Was Freddie bound when you left him?" Bert asked.

"Yes. His hands were tied in front of him, and his feet were roped together."

As the Bobbseys looked for footprints to see where the boys had gone, they heard a rustling.

"Drop down!" Bert ordered. "They may be coming back."

But Bert's intention of jumping out and grabbing the bullies was short-lived. For into view came Charlie Mason, a good-looking boy with large brown eyes and a pleasant smile. Charlie was Bert's best friend. Nan and Bert rose to their feet, and Snap and Waggo bounded up to Charlie, whom they liked.

"Hi, Charlie!" the twins called.

"Hello."

"How did you know we were here?" Bert asked.

"I just stopped at your house. What's up?"

Bert told him. "We're trying to figure out where Danny and Jack took Freddie."

"I have an idea," Charlie said.

"Where?"

"Danny and Jack's hideout shack in the woods!"

"Good hunch, Charlie. Let's go!"

The boys knew where Danny's hideout was located. They had discovered it some time before, and Danny did not like this.

Now, with Teddy and Nan trailing behind, Bert and Charlie hurried toward the hideout with the two dogs. The shack was in a woods to one side of town, about a quarter of a mile away.

As they neared the place Nan cried out, "Two boys are coming out of the woods."

"Leaping catfish!" Charlie exclaimed. "Danny and Jack!"

The two bullies must have spied the Bobbseys and their friends, for they scooted back into the fringe of trees and ran in the opposite direction.

"Stop!" Bert called out, racing after them.

But Danny and Jack kept on. "After them, Snap—Waggo!" Bert cried out.

The two dogs, yelping and barking, ranged ahead of the three searchers. Soon the animals were far beyond the children. Bert and Charlie put on a burst of speed, leaving Nan with Teddy.

"There they are!" cried Bert suddenly, and called out to them, "Where's Freddie?"

The fleeing bullies turned about for a moment. They looked frightened as they saw the dogs nearing them.

A short distance ahead was a stream. "Jump it!" Danny called to Jack. "We can throw the dogs off the scent that way."

But the two boys could not make it. They jumped, but landed two feet from the opposite side and fell forward on their faces. Bert called off Waggo and Snap. Then he and Charlie waded in. As the bullies got to the bank of the stream, they knew it was no use running. Bert had them cornered.

"What did you do with Freddie?" Bert demanded.

"We don't know anything about him," Danny said as the water dripped from his clothes.

Jack looked sheepish but said nothing. By this time Nan and Teddy had come up.

"You'd better tell us the truth," Nan cried out.

A cunning look came over Danny's face. "Huh! You think you're so honest and all that. Your father's friend out West is a gyp."

"A gyp?" Nan asked, puzzled.

"You know what I mean," Danny answered. "We heard everything when we were back of the garage, didn't we, Jack?"

"Dad's friend is a gyppo operator for a lumber company, and that's not bad," said Bert. He cocked his fists. "Tell me where my brother is, or I'll let you have it!" he exclaimed.

Jack, crestfallen, looked at his friend Danny. "Aw, I guess we've had enough," he said. "Why don't you tell 'em where the kid went?"

Without looking directly at Bert, Danny said, "Freddie's in the lot back of my house."

"Not now, he isn't," Bert declared. "We looked there. Come on! Where is he?"

"If he's not there, he must have got away by himself," Danny said.

"He's right," Jack nodded.

"You'd better be telling the truth," Bert stated.

As Danny and Jack stomped off, Bert and Charlie decided to take a look at the hideout just to make sure Freddie was not there. They did not see him.

"Maybe we missed Freddie at the lot because he headed home by another route," Bert reasoned as they emerged from the woods.

"Let's check at home," Nan suggested.

The children reached the street in a few minutes. They had not gone far when Nan suddenly noticed the Bobbsey station wagon coming down the street. They raced toward it, waving their arms. Mr. and Mrs. Bobbsey were in the front seat, and back of them sat Flossie—and Freddie!

"Oh, he's safe!" Nan cried out.

The four children climbed in and learned that Danny *had* been right. Freddie had freed himself and gone home. A few minutes later Charlie, then Teddy were dropped at their homes.

Nan said to Freddie, "Please tell us everything that happened!"

Her small brother showed some faint red marks on his wrists and described how he had been tied up. Then Freddie added, "Danny and Jack said 'the boss' was a clever fellow."

"Who?"

"The boss," Freddie repeated. "The boss doesn't want Daddy to go to Silver Creek."

"So that's it!" Bert said. "Nan, do you suppose he's the man we saw talking with Danny and Jack?" He told his parents about the stranger.

Mr. Bobbsey looked very thoughtful. "This mystery is getting bigger right here in Lakeport."

"I'll say it is, Dad," Bert continued. "If anybody is trying to stop you from going to Silver Creek—"

His father smiled and said he appreciated his children's loyalty, but he warned them not to get into any danger on his account.

"We'll be careful," Bert promised.

When the Bobbseys walked into their kitchen, Dinah said, "I do declare. Just as soon as you leave the house a special 'mergency comes up."

"What kind of an emergency?" Mr. Bobbsey asked.

"A long-distance call from the West Coast, Mr. Bobbsey."

The twins were now more excited than ever. Was the gyppo lumberman running into more trouble and appealing to their father for help?

"Did the person leave his name?" Mr. Bobbsey asked.

"No, but the long-distance operator left her number."

Nan, excited, eagerly volunteered to phone the operator. She did this, and the caller on the West Coast was contacted. Nan handed the receiver to her father.

Mr. Bobbsey wore a concerned look as he started to speak, but as the conversation continued, his face broke into a broad smile. "Yes, Mr. Hunter. Thank you so much, sir," he said. "My family will be delighted."

When he hung up, Mrs. Bobbsey was as keenly interested as the twins to learn what Mr. Hunter had said.

"I can tell it's something special," Flossie cried, throwing her arms around her father's neck. "I can tell, Daddy, by your funny look."

For a moment Mr. Bobbsey grinned teasingly at his family. Then he said, "You've never heard news like this before!"

He explained that the call was from the president of the country's largest lumber company. "It seems that the Bobbsey company has sold more lumber than any other dealer in this area, so we've won a prize."

For a moment the twins' excited cries drowned out their father's voice. "What's the prize?" they demanded.

"Our whole family," Mr. Bobbsey went on, "has been invited to visit a tree farm out West, with all our expenses paid!"

CHAPTER IV

A SLIM CLUE

"DAD, that's keen!" Bert exclaimed. "A trip out West!"

Mrs. Bobbsey hugged her husband, and Nan planted a kiss on his cheek. Freddie turned two somersaults.

"Dad," Nan said excitedly, "now we can help your friend, Mr. Everett, solve his mystery!"

"That's right. All of us can."

Flossie said she would be glad to see the gyppo outfit. "I want to tell Susie!" she exclaimed.

The little girl ran from the house and down the street to tell Susie Larker, her special playmate, of their good fortune.

Susie, a bright-eyed little girl of six who looked much like Flossie herself, was skipping rope on the sidewalk outside her home. After listening to Flossie's news, she cocked her head. "You said a tree farm?"

"That's what Daddy calls it," Flossie replied.

"Do you mean the farmer grows them like food?" Susie giggled.

"Maybe," her little friend replied. "I'll write and tell you," she promised.

By the end of that day the whole neighborhood knew of the wonderful forest adventure that the Bobbsey family was planning. Sam and Dinah seemed to be as excited as the children.

"Now you all be careful of the big bears, won't you?" Dinah begged Freddie and Flossie when they came to say good night to her in the kitchen.

"Oh, we will," Flossie promised.

Freddie then handed her a glass jar of insects that glowed in the dark. "Dinah, will you please let my lightning bugs go free?" he asked. "I won't need them any more."

The kindly colored woman took the jar outdoors. After she had released the bugs, she went to look for her husband. She found Sam talking with Mr. and Mrs. Bobbsey and the older twins on the front porch.

"We're just talking about our trip, Dinah," Mrs. Bobbsey said. "And why don't you and Sam take a little vacation while we're gone?"

Sam and Dinah were happy to hear this.

"We'll do it," said Sam. "And good luck on your trip. Are you all going to fly?"

"Yes. First to Chicago, then we'll change to a larger plane. After landing in Billings, Montana, we fly on to Seattle, Washington."

Mr. Bobbsey added that from there they would drive to Silver Creek, sixty miles southeast of Seattle, where they had been invited to stay at Mr. Everett's farm.

"Oh, I thought he was a lumberman," Sam remarked. "Is he a farmer, too?"

Mr. Bobbsey explained that many lumbermen on the West Coast commuted to their jobs in the forest every day. A lot of them lived on small farms and earned extra money from their fruits and vegetables.

Freddie and Flossie were so excited by the thought of the plane ride that before breakfast next morning, Freddie suggested a game of airplanes to Flossie.

The little fellow ran back upstairs and returned shortly with a handful of miniature planes. "Here," he said to his twin, handing her several. "We'll make believe the living room rug is the United States, and we'll fly our planes over it."

The younger twins busied themselves doing this for several minutes. Then Flossie said,

"Let's have some clouds in the sky, Freddie."

"How?"

"My bubble blower will make lovely clouds."

"Great idea," Freddie said. "Get it, Flossie."

His sister hurried from the room and soon returned with a cup of warm, soapy water and her bubble blower. A few minutes later she had strings of bubbles floating lazily about the room. Freddie darted his little planes in and out among the make-believe clouds.

"Whee—this is fun!" he exclaimed.

Finally Dinah's voice called, "Breakfast is ready!"

Flossie had just blown a huge bubble, as large as Freddie's head, toward the door to the dining room. Quickly Freddie caught it on the end of his nose and marched to the table.

Pop! it went, spattering the soapy water all over his face. Everyone laughed.

After the meal was over, and Mr. Bobbsey was preparing to leave for work, the telephone rang. The call was from Sam Johnson. It was his custom to open the lumberyard early in the morning. Sam sounded excited as Mr. Bobbsey spoke to him.

"Our two big lumber trucks?" Mr. Bobbsey gasped. "You say someone damaged them during the night? I'll be right down!"

Mr. Bobbsey relayed the bad news to his family. "Why, that's terrible!" Mrs. Bobbsey burst out. "Who could have done it?"

Nan, upset, looked at her father. "Oh, I hope that horrid man who spoke to Danny and Jack isn't trying to keep us from making the trip, Daddy."

"I do, too," Mr. Bobbsey said. "Please call the police, Mary. Have them send a man over to the yard. I'll go there right away." He hurried out to the garage.

As their mother went to phone headquarters, Bert and Nan ran after their father and begged to ride with him.

"All right," Mr. Bobbsey said. "Jump in."

Halfway to the lumberyard, Bert noticed a car keeping about half a block behind them. "Dad," he said, "I think that driver is following us on purpose."

The twins' father slowed down and so did the other car. When Mr. Bobbsey increased his speed the vehicle behind did also.

"I'll find out if he's following me!" Mr. Bobbsey exclaimed angrily. He turned sharply into the next driveway and stopped his car.

"Good!" Nan said. "Now we'll chase him!"

But the driver of the car behind had no intention of being followed himself. Pulling his hat low and partly covering his face with one hand, he put on a burst of speed. He passed the Bobbseys and was out of sight before Mr. Bobbsey could pick up the trail.

"He was trailing us for sure," the twins' father said as they continued toward the lumberyard. "But why?"

By the time the Bobbseys drove into the lumberyard, Sam was pacing up and down at the entrance. He was waving his arms excitedly.

"Right over here," he said.

When Mr. Bobbsey stopped the car, the twins

hopped out. They followed Sam and their father to the metal garage which housed the company trucks. The hoods of two of them were up, revealing marks where the motors had been struck, apparently by a sledge hammer.

"This is senseless damage," Mr. Bobbsey said.

"Do you suppose someone did it for a mean joke, Dad?" Bert asked.

"No," his father replied. Mr. Bobbsey said the vandal would have had to scale the high fence surrounding the lumberyard and get out the same way, carrying the large hammer.

"You mean," said Bert, "that whoever did it wasn't fooling."

"Yes, son."

"Then," said Nan, "we ought to look for clues. Come on, Bert."

The twins walked around the yard looking for anything which the vandal might have dropped by mistake. "I guess there aren't any footprints," Bert deduced, "because this ground is so sun-baked they wouldn't show up."

A few moments later, though, he did find the spot where the person probably had scaled the fence. On the ground was the mark of a hammerhead. The heavy tool no doubt had been tossed over first.

"If the man dropped anything," Nan commented, "it should be right here."

The children scoured the area and finally Nan cried out, "Look, Bert!" She picked up a thin, blue plastic object.

"What is it?"

"A spoon," his twin replied. The two examined the object carefully.

"Good night! Look at the lettering, Nan. *'Trans U. S. Airways.'* "

"Then whoever dropped it," his sister reasoned, "may have been a passenger on that airline—or works for it."

"Right," said Bert. "Let's telephone the airline office and see what we can find out."

After telling their father of their find, the twins hurried into the lumberyard office. Bert dialed the airline number. The woman who answered said yes, Trans U. S. Airways had put such spoons into service only the month before on their large coast-to-coast aircraft.

Bert thanked her. Then he and Nan raced to their father with the information. "Don't you see, Dad," Nan said excitedly, "the man came from the West Coast and not long ago, either!"

"Maybe his fingerprints are on the spoon," Mr. Bobbsey suggested. "Show it to the police when they get here."

A young officer named Murphy arrived in a prowl car a few moments later and heard the story. Then Bert asked him whether the plastic spoon contained fingerprints that would help identify the vandal.

The policeman brought a fingerprint kit from his car, tested the spoon and then shook his head. "There are several persons' prints on it," he said, "but they're too mixed up to be of any use. Well, let's see the trucks."

Mr. Bobbsey led the policeman to the garage. After seeing the damage, he asked, "Did you find any clues here?"

Bert and Nan began to look about immediately, and the Bobbsey boy crawled under one of the trucks.

"Hey, I found something," he said, wriggling out between the two front wheels.

"What is it?" Mr. Bobbsey asked.

Bert held out a penknife, and they all looked at it. On a metal plate on the handle of the knife were inscribed the initials J. W.

"Do you know anyone with those initials?" Officer Murphy asked.

Bert hated to tell, but finally he said, "Yes. Jack Westley!"

"Do you think he might have done this?" the officer asked.

Nan spoke up quickly, saying that she did not think Jack was mean enough to wreck a motor. The policeman, after hearing about Danny's friend, agreed with Nan. But he added:

"If I were you I'd talk to him, anyway. Since you know him already, you might be able to find out more facts than I could."

"We'll try," Bert said. "We'll question Jack and report to you."

Sam drove Bert and Nan to the street where Jack Westley lived. They confronted him as he came out the front door of his home.

"Is this your knife, Jack?" Bert asked, holding it up for the boy to see.

Jack's glance went from the knife to Bert and Nan. "It used to be mine," he confessed.

"What do you mean 'used to be'?" Bert asked.

"I sold it."

"To whom?" Nan asked.

In return, Jack managed a feeble smile. "That's none of your business."

"Yes, it is," Bert said, and told about the damaged trucks. Then he added, hoping to trap Jack into an admission, "I know whom you sold the knife to—that stranger from the West Coast you were talking to."

Jack's mouth fell open in surprise, and he looked frightened.

CHAPTER V

A WORRISOME CALLER

JACK WESTLEY was so alarmed that for a moment he could not speak. He started to say something, then hesitated.

"Then I'm right!" Bert declared. "You did sell your knife to that man, and he is from the West Coast."

Jack shifted uneasily. "Ask Danny," he said. "Danny knows more about everything than I do."

"Okay. But what about this knife?" Bert asked. "Do you want to give it back to the man?"

"No!" Jack shouted.

"Then we'll turn the knife over to the police," said Bert.

Jack did not even argue. He turned and raced into his house, the screen door slamming behind him.

Bert and Nan smiled and went back to their car. At once Sam asked, "How did you two detectives make out?"

"Not bad," Bert replied. "We just found out that the man who's so interested in us really did come from the West Coast."

The twins felt that they should tell the police about this immediately. Sam drove them back to the lumberyard. Fortunately Officer Murphy was still there. After hearing the story about the knife, he took it and said he would try to find out more about the suspicious man.

A moment later Sam called out, "Here comes the tow truck!"

A big wrecker backed into the driveway of the lumberyard. The front of one of the damaged trucks was hitched to the rear of the wrecker to be towed off to a repair garage.

"I'll come right back for the other one," the driver said, as he pulled away.

The policeman had finished his investigation and said he would go back to headquarters.

"The department will keep an extra lookout around your lumberyard, Mr. Bobbsey," he promised.

Bert and Nan stayed at the lumberyard until nearly lunchtime, hoping to hear a report on the vandal. But none came.

They drove home with their father. As the

car pulled into the rear of the driveway, Nan whispered:

"Look at Flossie and Freddie!"

The small twins had just finished planting a spot three feet square at the end of a flower bed near the house. Tiny sprigs of maple stood up in rows four inches apart. They had been well watered.

"Isn't that pretty?" Nan said, as Mr. Bobbsey stopped.

"We got these in the woods," Freddie said.

"Isn't our farm bee-yoo-ti-ful?" Flossie asked as she danced around and clapped her hands. "We're going to play that a nice woods fairy will wave a wand and make our little tree farm into a big forest."

Mr. Bobbsey smiled when he heard this, and Freddie giggled. "Oh, there aren't any woods fairies," he said.

"Well, we can make believe, can't we, Freddie?" Flossie said.

"I'll be the woods fairy," said Freddie suddenly. He spread his arms and pretended he had wings. He picked up a stick with which Waggo had been playing. "This is my wand, and I'll change our tree farm. Watch!"

Freddie waved the "wand" over the sprigs of maple. "Abacadabra, abacadabra," the boy intoned. "I want a *big forest.*"

Seeing that nothing happened, Flossie held a hand to her mouth to stifle a giggle.

"Don't laugh," her twin said. "I haven't had much practice being a woods fairy."

"Go ahead, try again!" Flossie encouraged him.

This time Freddie put more into the act. Besides waving the wand, he danced around, trying to do some steps that Flossie did in dancing school. But suddenly he slipped in the mud on the edge of the freshly watered tree farm.

"Fredd-ee!" Flossie called. "Be careful!"

But Freddie's feet took a skid, and he landed with a *splat* right on top of the little maple sprigs.

"Oh!" Flossie wailed. "You've ruined our tree farm!"

As Freddie struggled to his feet, he said, "I'll replant the trees."

Bert and Nan helped them, and soon the tiny tree farm looked very nice again. Then Freddie went to take a bath and change his clothes. As he passed his mother in the hall, she said, "Oh, my goodness!"

With a grin, Freddie replied, "I didn't get muddy on the front side of me!" His mother laughed merrily.

By the time Dinah was ready to serve luncheon to the family, Freddie appeared, clean and neat. The table talk was all about tree farming and the Bobbseys' trip to the West Coast. The twins' father said that the chief crop of trees out there was Douglas firs.

"They're the giants of the forest," he said, "and are nearly as tall as the redwoods which grow in California."

"Are there dangerous things in the woods, like snakes?" Flossie asked.

Her father laughed. "Strangely enough," he said, "there are no snakes on the western slopes of the mountains in Washington. There's too much rain for them, I guess."

"Goody," Flossie remarked. "Then I don't have to worry."

Mrs. Bobbsey remarked that even the bears out there seemed friendly and would not bother people if they were not disturbed themselves. Then the twins' mother asked how many things her children could name which were made from wood.

"Oh, that would be a good guessing game!" Nan said as Dinah cleared away the dishes before serving dessert.

"Let me guess first," Freddie said. He thought for a moment. "Trees are good for making tree houses."

"And for holding up birds' nests," Flossie said with a twinkle in her eyes.

"Come now, let's be serious," suggested Nan.

The children took turns naming things made from wood—houses, furniture, boats, and paper.

"I know another one," Nan remarked. "Dresses!"

Freddie raised his eyebrows. "You mean paper-doll dresses?"

Nan chuckled. "No, Freddie. Dresses for girls to wear and also draperies."

"I know one," said Bert. "Rayon. That's made from wood pulp."

Mr. Bobbsey was about to tell the children how this was done when suddenly the front door-bell rang. Presently Dinah, who answered it, came to say that Mr. Taylor, a lawyer, was calling to see Mr. Bobbsey. Through the doorway to the living room the children could see a short, thin man with a sallow complexion.

The twins' father arose and went to speak to Mr. Taylor.

The caller stated his errand at once. "Mr. Bobbsey," he said, "I represent a client who wishes to buy your share in the gyppo lumber company in Washington."

Mr. Bobbsey was taken aback by the offer. "Who is it that wants to purchase my share?" the twins' father asked.

"I can't divulge the name of my client," Mr. Taylor said smugly.

"Well, Mr. Taylor," said Mr. Bobbsey, "I don't want to sell my interest in the Washington company."

"My client is willing to offer you a very good price," Mr. Taylor said.

"I'm not selling," the twins' father said pleasantly, but in a firm voice.

The lawyer, who had just opened his brief case, snapped it shut. "Very well," he said, rising and starting for the door. "But you'll be sorry, Mr. Bobbsey! Very sorry!"

CHAPTER VI

THE CATSKINNER

AFTER the caller left, the twins and their mother went quickly into the living room. From a window they watched Mr. Taylor hasten down the walk, step into his car and drive off.

"He sure was in a hurry to buy your interest in the business, Dad," Bert remarked. "Why all the big rush?"

Mr. Bobbsey said he was as much perplexed as Bert.

Flossie was a little frightened, remembering the man's words. "Mr. Taylor isn't going to hurt you, Daddy, is he?"

"Don't worry about that, Fat Fairy," her father said, patting his small daughter. "Mr. Taylor certainly made a threat. However, I can't think of any reason why he should try to harm me."

All this time Nan had been thinking hard. Looking at her father, she asked him whether his and Mr. Everett's company owned anything besides tools and equipment.

"Yes, we own some land," was the reply.

"How much?" Bert joined in, surprised to hear this.

Mr. Bobbsey revealed that he and Mr. Everett together owned a hundred-acre timber tract on which they had started a logging operation several years before.

"But now this tract has all been cut and replanted," Mr. Bobbsey added.

His wife suggested that it was probably the land which Mr. Taylor's client wanted.

In reply, Mr. Bobbsey shrugged. "It really hasn't any great value now," he said, "and will not have any for many years to come. Not until the new timber crop is ready."

"But maybe it has a *hidden* value, Dad," Nan suggested.

"You mean something in the ground?"

"Yes."

Mr. Bobbsey pursed his lips. Then he said, "I'm going to telephone Mr. Everett and find out if he has been approached, too."

Mrs. Bobbsey added, "Possibly Mr. Everett may know why Mr. Taylor's client wants to buy the business."

"That's right," Mr. Bobbsey agreed.

It took only a few minutes for him to contact

his partner's farm on the West Coast. Fortunately Mr. Everett had returned from the
woods. He spoke loudly enough for the others
to hear.

Mr. Everett was surprised to learn that such
an offer had been made to Mr. Bobbsey—par-
ticularly because a similar proposal had been
made to him that very morning!

"A local lawyer named Berryman called on
me," Mr. Everett explained. "He said that you
were eager to sell your share."

"Not at all!" Mr. Bobbsey answered, frown-
ing. "What did you tell him?"

"That I wasn't interested in the offer."

"I'm glad of that," said Mr. Bobbsey. "I'm
afraid our problem is getting worse. Perhaps
we can clear it up when I visit you with my
family."

"I hope so, Dick. And get here as soon as
you can."

The westerner now lowered his voice, so the
twins could not hear what he was saying. But
after the phone conversation was over, Mr.
Bobbsey reported that Mr. Everett was still having troubles at the gyppo operation but that he
had hired another bucker and a catskinner.

Hearing this Flossie looked startled. "A catskinner?" she asked. "Oh, no!" and ran out of
the room. She returned in a moment, holding a

black cat protectively under her arm. "If Mr. Everett ever comes to visit us," she said, "I'll hide Snoop right away. I don't want my nice old pussycat skinned."

Mr. Bobbsey chuckled and explained that in lumber country a catskinner is a man who operates a caterpillar tractor.

Flossie hunched her shoulders. "Don't tease me any more. I know tractors don't have *real* caterpillars on them, just funny, big tires they call caterpillars."

"Right," said her father. "And a bucker is a fellow who saws trees at their proper length for transportation to the mill." Flossie felt better and let Snoop go.

After the twins' father had returned to work, they went outside to tidy their yard. The lawn had to be cut and outdoor toys put into the garage for safekeeping during the children's absence on the trip.

Bert and Nan took down the badminton net. Freddie and Flossie picked up tiny pails and shovels that lay scattered about their sandbox.

With all the toys in their proper places, Bert and Nan took turns using the power mower. Freddie and Flossie got clippers and trimmed the grass along the walk.

As they finished Dinah stepped into the yard to admire their work. "Now isn't that scrumptious?" the plump, jolly cook exclaimed merrily. "You children are a big help."

As Bert put the lawnmower away Flossie discovered Nan's roller skates beside the porch and started to put them into the garage.

Just then Dinah said, "Now for all your good work, children, what would you like me to do for you?" Dinah, of course, expected the twins to ask for her special chocolate chip cookies or perhaps some homemade ice cream.

Flossie was the first one to speak up. With a twinkle in her eyes, she said, "There's something I've always wanted you to do, Dinah."

"What's that, honey lamb?" Dinah asked.

"I want to see you roller-skate!" Flossie held the pair of skates toward Dinah.

The cook raised her hands, shook her head, and declared, "Roller-skate? Why, child alive, I haven't roller-skated since I was a little girl. And I was a lot thinner then. I don't think I could do it any more."

"Certainly you could," Nan said. She thought it would be fun to watch Dinah try it anyhow and said so.

Dinah continued to laugh and say, "No!" while the Bobbseys begged her to try the stunt.

Finally Flossie looked up at Dinah pleadingly. "Please do it, Dinah, 'cause we won't have any more fun with you for a long time. We'll be away."

This made the cook look sad. "All right, I'll do it," she said, "under one condition."

"What's that?" Bert asked.

"I'd like to pin a pillow onto me," Dinah said, "just in case I should sit down unexpected-like."

Nan hurried into the house and returned with a large sofa pillow and two safety pins. She pinned the pillow to the strings at the back of Dinah's apron. Then the cook sat on the back steps while Bert adjusted the roller skates to her shoes.

Dinah chuckled all the while, complaining that if she laughed any more she would be too weak to stand up.

Finally the skates were in place, and Dinah stood up, holding onto Bert and Nan. Then she gingerly slid a foot forward on the concrete sidewalk that led to the front of the house.

"There!" Nan cried gleefully as they reached the front, and they let go of her. "You're doing fine, Dinah!"

As the cook was about to try to skate alone, Sam drove past in a lumber truck. His eyes ballooned as he spied his wife on roller skates. The truck brakes squealed and Sam stopped.

"Lawsy me, Dinah Johnson!" he cried out.
"What's goin' on?"

Confused, embarrassed, and laughing all at
once, Dinah lost her balance.

Plop! She landed on the pillow. The children
rushed over to her.

"You're a good sport, Dinah," Nan said, as
she and Bert tried to help the cook get up. But
they could not budge her.

Sam jumped down to assist, and Freddie and

Flossie joined in. They got Dinah to her feet, chuckling and puffing, but as soon as they let go of her she started to sit down again.

"It's no use with these here skates on," she said, so Freddie and Flossie removed them.

"But it was fun, wasn't it, Dinah?" Flossie asked.

Dinah rolled her brown eyes. "Well, that's a matter of opinion, honey child." She grinned. "I think I'm much better at baking cookies."

Still chuckling, she took the pillow and went into the house.

Before Sam drove off he told Bert and Nan that this was one of the repaired trucks. The second one was due out of the garage next morning.

"The police are still lookin' for the vandal who used a hammer on 'em," Sam said, and added that so far they had no further clue to the person other than the knife.

Next morning at breakfast Flossie made everyone laugh by telling of a dream she had had about Dinah climbing a tall tree on roller skates. "She was going up to give some baby squirrels a plate of cookies!"

"And I dreamed," Freddie spoke up, "that a big catskinner came here and took Snap and Waggo. He wanted them to help him drive his caterpillar tractor."

His twin giggled. "Maybe they could. They're very smart dogs!"

When Bert finished eating, he asked to be excused from the table. As his mother nodded, he said, "I want to go over to Charlie Mason's. I promised to lend him my tennis racket while we're gone. Are there any errands to do?"

His mother said, no, not at the moment. Bert ran to the garage to get his racket, but returned seconds later, a shocked look on his face.

"All our toys are gone!" he shouted. "Come and look!"

All the Bobbseys hastened to the garage. Everyone gasped, and Freddie cried out in dismay, "My pogo stick's missing!"

Bert noticed an open window. "Someone climbed in there! It was jimmied open!" he exclaimed.

The children quickly discovered that among the things which had been taken were Bert's tennis racket, Flossie's doll and doll carriage, and a bow and arrow set belonging to Nan.

"I'm surprised Waggo and Snap didn't hear the thief and bark," Mrs. Bobbsey said, but it was discovered that both dogs had been sleeping in the kitchen during the night.

"Who could have been mean enough to take our toys?" Nan asked as she looked around.

Bert instantly thought of Jack and Danny, but Nan did not believe the bullies would dare do anything like this.

Freddie had stepped out of the garage to search for his pogo stick just in case the burglar might have dropped it. Suddenly the little boy saw Jack Westley walking down the street. He called to his brother and sisters.

The twins ran out and confronted Jack. They told him of the theft, and Bert asked, "Do you know anything about it?"

"Of course not! And say, if you think I did it, you're crazy!" Suddenly Jack burst out, "I know who probably did do it! That man. And he's trying to put the blame on Danny and me!"

"What man?" Bert asked. "The one from the West Coast?"

"Yes. I don't know his name."

"Who does, then?" Bert asked.

Jack said that Danny might know and added, "He's the one who got the two dollars!"

CHAPTER VII

HIGH CLIMBER FREDDIE

"SO DANNY got some money," Bert said. "For what?"

Jack stared at the ground and kicked a pebble. "I'm not going to be a squealer," he muttered, looking unhappy.

"Then we'll ask Danny ourselves," Bert told him. Jack hurried off.

After telling their parents what had happened, the older twins hopped on their bicycles and pedaled toward Danny's house. Bert rang the doorbell, and Mrs. Rugg answered.

"Hello," she said. "Are you looking for Danny?"

"Yes."

"I'm sorry, but he's in his room and can't come down."

Bert and Nan were sure Danny was being punished. They wondered if it had anything to do with the mysterious man.

"It's very important, Mrs. Rugg," said Nan. "Really it is."

"Well, all right. I'll call him." She went to the foot of the stairs. "Danny! You may come down now."

Danny hurried to the first floor. He was amazed to see Bert and Nan and did not even say hello. "What do you want?" he asked.

The Bobbseys would have preferred that Mrs. Rugg leave, but she stayed, so finally Bert said, "Danny, we came to find out why that man gave you two dollars and who he is."

Hanging his head, Danny replied, "I don't have to tell you."

"But you'll tell *me*," his mother said. "What's this all about?"

Grudgingly Danny admitted that he had received the two dollars from a man who said he was "the boss."

"He was looking for the Bobbseys' house when he met Jack and me," Danny explained.

"Is he the one who bought Jack's knife?" Bert asked him.

"Yes."

"And the one who doesn't want us to go out West? Freddie heard you say so."

"Uh-huh," Danny replied.

Mrs. Rugg, startled, interrupted. "What did that man ask you and Jack to do?"

Her son said that he had made many inquir-
ies about the Bobbsey family.

"What did you tell him?" Nan said quickly.
Under further questioning Danny confessed
that he had told the stranger of Mr. Bobbsey's
proposed trip to Silver Creek.

Mrs. Rugg's face was stern as she listened to
her son. "Then what did the man say?" she
queried him sharply.

"He said, 'How would you like to spoil that
trip for Mr. Bobbsey?' I thought this would be
a good idea."

"How naughty! Why?" Mrs. Rugg asked.

"Just to get even for what the Bobbseys did
to me," Danny said.

Nan spoke up quickly. "It was your own
fault, Danny."

"Well, never mind whose fault it was," Mrs.
Rugg said impatiently. "Why did you take the
two dollars from this man, Danny?"

Looking worried, the boy confessed that "the
boss" had paid him two dollars to capture Freddie. In addition, he had bought Jack Westley's
old knife for fifty cents. When Mrs. Rugg told
her son to describe the man, Danny said he was
slender, dark-haired, and had a thin face with
rather large ears.

"You should never have done such a thing,"
Mrs. Rugg admonished her son. "In the future

I want you to stay away from that man. And never *never* accept any money from strangers. Promise?"

Danny promised. Then Nan asked him if he would be on the lookout for the stranger and let them know if he was still around. Danny did not answer yes or no. Bert mentioned the toys stolen from the Bobbseys' garage. Danny denied knowing anything about them. Then he disappeared around the side of the house.

The twins mounted their bicycles and pedaled homeward.

"What puzzles me," Bert said, "is why this man wants to keep Dad from making his trip."

"Yes, and now that we're all going," Nan added, "do you think he'll try to stop the whole family?"

"I sure hope not," said Bert, worried. "Say, I think I know why 'the boss' bought Jack's penknife."

"Why?"

"So he could leave it near the damaged trucks and put the blame on Jack Westley."

"He's really bad," Nan commented.

The moment the twins arrived home Bert called the police from the hall phone. He gave them the description of the stranger.

"Thank you. This will help us find him," the officer said.

After Bert put down the phone, he ran into the living room and nearly tripped on a large open book. It was a volume from the set of encyclopedia.

"Hey, what's this?" he said aloud.

Dinah, coming in, told him Flossie and Freddie had left it there. The book was open to a chapter on lumbering. One page contained a picture of a high climber with spiked shoes and a safety belt. He was near the top of a giant fir tree.

"Take a look at this, Nan," Bert called to his twin, who was on her way upstairs. She came back.

"I wouldn't want that kind of a job," Nan said, laughing, after gazing at the climber.

As Bert returned the volume to the bookcase, the telephone rang. Instantly the twins wondered whether the police, using the description of the stranger, had captured him.

Nan lifted the phone. On the other end of the line was a baby sitter at Teddy Blake's house. Her voice was frantic.

"Hurry over, all of you, please. Freddie's in trouble!"

"What's the matter?" Nan asked anxiously, but the woman had hung up.

"Mother, Mother!" Nan cried out. Mrs. Bobbsey did not answer.

"Your mother's at a Garden Club meeting," Dinah told her. "What's troublin' you, Nan?"

Quickly the girl explained to both Dinah and Bert.

"We'd better get over there pronto!" Bert said.

He dashed from the house, followed by his sister and Dinah. The Blake home was not far away. In less than two minutes the three ran into the back yard. Teddy, Flossie, and the baby sitter were standing at the foot of an old pine tree, looking up.

Twenty-five feet up the trunk was Freddie!

He was strapped to the tree by a belt which Bert and Nan guessed was an old one of their father's.

"Honey child, come down here right away!" Dinah ordered.

"He can't," the baby sitter said.

Freddie looked at those below him. His lips quivered as he tried to be brave. "I can go up," he called, "but I can't get down."

"Yes, he shinned up all by himself," Flossie said, proud of her twin.

Bert called out for his brother to stay quietly where he was. "I'll get a ladder right away, Freddie," he said.

Teddy directed Bert to a ladder which hung

on a rack in the garage. Nan helped him, and together they put it against the old pine tree.

"Oh, it doesn't reach far enough," Nan said.

Bert climbed up, but he could not touch his small brother.

"Oh, get me down!" Freddie wailed.

"In just a minute," said Bert, coming down again.

He ran into the Blake home and dialed the operator. "Please call the fire department," he said. "Tell them to come here quick!" He gave the address.

Three minutes later came the sound of sirens. The hook and ladder was the first to arrive at the Blakes', with the firemen pulling on their rubber coats and caps. They ran into the yard.

"Where's the fire?" one of the men asked.

"No fire." Nan pointed to the top of the tree. "My little brother's stuck up there."

Seeing this, the firemen took off their rubber coats. Then they backed the hook and ladder into the Blakes' driveway. A fireman stood on one end of the long ladder as it lay flat on top of the truck.

Then *whirr whirr whirr,* a motor started and the ladder began rising into the air. As everyone cheered, the firemen maneuvered the ladder against the tree where Freddie hung.

The firemen maneuvered the ladder against the tree
where Freddie hung

In a few seconds the frightened boy was loosened from the tree and in the fireman's arms. Slowly the ladder came down.

"Thanks for saving me," Freddie said, when he was on the ground again.

"Glad to be of help," the fireman replied, smiling. "This is the first time I ever rescued a bird boy!"

"I'm going to be a fireman someday and rescue people," Freddie told him.

"I see," the man said. "I thought maybe you were going to be a steeplejack."

"Not me," declared Freddie. "I don't like hanging from high places."

All the Bobbseys went to bed early that night so they would be fresh for the start of their trip in the morning.

At the breakfast table, Dinah beamed as she served piping hot bacon and eggs. "Eat well," she said, " 'cause you got a long ride ahead of you."

When the meal was over, the suitcases were put in the car, and Sam drove the family to the Lakeport airfield. The Bobbseys climbed into a small plane bound for Chicago. The craft soon was flying high over fields and rivers and, some time later, landed at the busy air terminal in Chicago.

The baggage was quickly transferred to a

large Trans U. S. Airways plane. Mr. Bobbsey had secured reservations on the right side of the plane where there were rows of three seats. Mrs. Bobbsey sat with Freddie and Flossie. Bert and Nan were with their father just behind them. It was not long before the aircraft rose from the runway in a thundering roar and soared into the blue sky.

"Isn't this exciting?" Nan called into Bert's ear.

"It sure is."

Several minutes after they were airborne Bert turned his head to look about the airplane. It was filled with people.

The boy's gaze finally came to rest on a man seated on the aisle three seats behind him. Bert's heart gave a thump. The man was slender, dark-haired, and had a thin face with large ears!

"Nan, look back there—three seats behind!" he said excitedly.

Nan turned her head slowly to look at the man, who was reading a magazine. "Do you think he could be the one we're looking for?" Nan whispered.

"Maybe. I'm going to try to find out somehow."

The hostesses, meanwhile, were busy serving refreshments to the passengers. One of the young women, a pretty girl in a trim blue uniform, put a cup of coffee and a doughnut on a tray before the dark-haired man. He glanced up to see Bert and Nan looking at him.

The twins turned their heads quickly but peered back a short time later. The man had just poured cream into his coffee and stirred it with one of the airline's plastic spoons.

Then Nan saw something that made her gasp in surprise as she recalled the Trans U. S. Airways spoon found near the damaged lumber truck. The man wiped the spoon with his napkin and put it into his pocket!

CHAPTER VIII

AN EMBARRASSING SPILL

THIS man who saved airplane spoons and the mysterious Lakeport stranger must be the same person, Nan decided. Her heart beat wildly as she confided her suspicion to Bert and Mr. Bobbsey.

"I'll bet he is," said Bert. "Let's have a policeman talk to him as soon as we get to the airport!"

But his father was not for such hasty action. "You can't confront a man who only looks like the suspect, without real proof of his guilt. Besides, there are many people who save spoons from all over the world as souvenirs."

The twins knew their father was right, but they still wanted to be sure about the man.

"I wish we could talk to him," Nan whispered to her twin. "Then perhaps we could find out if he's guilty of damaging Dad's trucks."

"Right," said Bert. "And if he gave Danny money to scare us about Freddie."

Soon after lunch a chance presented itself. The stranger arose and strolled back to the lounge at the end of the plane. Quickly the older twins followed and took seats next to him.

The man had picked up a magazine and began turning the pages. Presently he came to an advertisement of a station wagon and paused to look at it.

"We have one like that," Bert spoke up pleasantly. After a pause he added, "Or maybe you know that already."

"How should I?" the stranger asked gruffly.

"Oh, don't you come from Lakeport?" Nan spoke up.

"No."

"But you visited there recently, didn't you? We thought we saw you on the street."

"You've got the wrong person."

"I'm sorry," said Bert. "A boy we know named Danny Rugg told us about a man who looks like you."

"What!"

"The man had a funny nickname," said Bert. The boy watched the stranger carefully as he added, "He called himself 'the boss.'"

The man showed no outward sign of alarm at the boy's remark. But Nan detected a vein in his forehead which throbbed angrily. Did this mean he was guilty or just annoyed?

"I'm not interested," he said curtly.

The twins, realizing they would learn nothing from the man, got up and started back to their seats. Halfway there they met one of the stewardesses, who was resting in a seat.

"Enjoying the trip?" she asked, smiling.

Nan said yes they were, then she queried, "Do you know the name of that man who's reading a magazine in the lounge? His regular seat is up there." She pointed it out.

The stewardess checked her passenger list. "Why, yes, his name is Radkin," she said.

"Is he from the West Coast?" Bert asked.

"The address here is New York City."

The twins thanked the stewardess and returned to their seats. "I guess we were wrong." Nan sighed.

At this moment Flossie turned around. "We invented a new game. Want to play it?" she said.

"Sure."

The young twins asked Bert and Nan to look out the window. The plane was now flying over the border of Wisconsin and Minnesota. Far below, the countryside was dotted with lakes.

"We look at the shape of the lakes," Flossie explained, "then we give them names."

"Oh, I see one over there," Freddie cried. "Don't you think it looks like an owl?"

"Yes! We'll call it Owl Lake!" Flossie said.

Nan and Bert immediately joined in the fun, and before long there were Cat, Mouse, Snake, Peach and Steeple Lakes.

Mrs. Bobbsey, overhearing the game, laughed. "The lakes have new names whether the people below know it or not!"

Finally Bert chuckled and said, "Say, there's a lake that looks like an ice cream soda."

"Even the water looks kind of brown like chocolate," Freddie remarked.

At the mention of a soda Flossie had run her tongue over her lips. "I'm thirsty," she told her mother.

"Would you like a cup of milk, honey?" Mrs. Bobbsey asked her.

"Oh, yes."

"Then suppose you walk back and ask the stewardness for some," Mrs. Bobbsey suggested.

Flossie arose and made her way down the aisle to the center of the plane where there was a small galley. The stewardess in charge gave Flossie a small carton of cold milk, which she drank at once. "Thank you," she said. "And may I have one for Freddie? He's my twin."

"Why, certainly, dear."

The young woman opened another carton

and handed it to Flossie, who started up the aisle. She had gone only a couple of steps when a lighted sign flashed over a door at the front of the plane: FASTEN SEAT BELTS.

At the same time the pilot's voice sounded over the loudspeaker. "This is your captain," he said in a deep, confident tone. "According to our radar we are approaching a storm area. It may be rough for a few minutes."

"Oh dear," thought Flossie, "I wonder if I can get to my seat in time."

She continued down the aisle, careful not to spill the milk, which she held in her right hand. Nan, watching her sister, motioned to Flossie to hurry. At the same moment she saw Mr. Radkin pass Flossie and return to his seat.

The little girl was halfway to her place when the plane dipped. She swayed, but regained her balance and started forward again. As she came opposite Mr. Radkin's chair, the plane zoomed upward.

"Oops!" cried Flossie, and she pitched sideways. The carton of milk flew into the air as the little girl grabbed for the seat. A split second later the milk landed in the man's lap!

Angrily he cried out, "Oh, you Bobbseys again!"

"Oh, I'm sorry!" Flossie apologized. "The p-plane is awful bumpy."

The stewardess, seeing what had happened,

grabbed a napkin and rushed forward. She
quickly handed it to Mr. Radkin, then led Flossie to her seat.

Just then the seat belt warning flashed off
and the ride became smooth again. Mr. and
Mrs. Bobbsey strolled back to the lounge.

Flossie told Freddie how she had tried to
bring him some milk and had spilled it on a
man. "He knows us," the little girl added.

Hearing this, Bert leaned forward. "What
makes you say that?" he asked, amazed.

" 'Cause he said," Flossie told him, " 'Oh, you Bobbseys again!' "

"You're sure?"

"Of course I'm sure."

Bert and Nan looked at each other. "Let's find out about this!" Bert said.

"I want to go, too," Freddie piped up.

In the end both sets of twins started down the aisle. Reaching Mr. Radkin's seat, they paused and Nan said, "I'm sorry my little sister spilled the milk. I hope it didn't leave a stain."

"No. It's all right."

Bert spoke up, "Flossie says you called us the Bobbseys. How do you know us?"

Mr. Radkin looked startled. "I guess I heard someone mention your name," he answered.

Nan asked quickly, "You mean in Lakeport?"

A tightness showed around Mr. Radkin's mouth. He looked toward the window and did not reply for several seconds. Then he said, "I heard it on the plane."

Nan realized that, as before, further questioning would be useless. Again the girl felt she might be wrong. As she and Bert turned away from Mr. Radkin, they noticed that Freddie and Flossie were talking to a pleasant-looking elderly man on the opposite side of the plane.

"Is this your first plane ride?" he was asking.

"Oh, no, we've had lots of rides," Freddie replied. "But this is the first one to Silver Creek."

"Really now," the man said, "isn't that interesting? I'd like to hear about it."

Before Nan and Bert had a chance to warn the younger twins not to tell too much, Freddie and Flossie were unfolding the story of their father's mystery on the West Coast.

Across the aisle, Mr. Radkin appeared to be dozing. But Nan wondered if he were really sleeping, or was he listening to the entire conversation?

The girl's interest suddenly was directed to the elderly man who was talking to the younger twins. Now he had Flossie on one knee and an arm about Freddie's shoulders.

"My, my, Silver Creek," he was saying.

"You've been there?" Flossie asked, looking up into the man's face.

"No. Unfortunately I've never had the time," he replied. "My grandmother came from there. My name's Wheeler, by the way."

"We have a grandmother, too," Freddie said, "only she lives back East."

Mr. Wheeler listened to the younger twins' chatter for a while, then he said, "If you Bobbsey twins like mysteries, how would you like to hear a mystery about my grandmother?"

"Oh, please tell us!" the children chorused.

CHAPTER IX

THIRTEEN DOTS

"MY GRANDMOTHER was involved in a deep, deep mystery," Mr. Wheeler began his story, as the twins crowded close to him in the plane. Across the aisle Mr. Radkin still seemed to be sound asleep.

Mr. Wheeler said that his grandmother, Mary Lou Wheeler, was only three years old and her brother Douglas two, when her family traveled across the Cascade Mountains in the state of Washington.

"Near Silver Creek they were attacked by Indians who were angry about having more white people travel through their land."

"Oh, how awful!" Flossie exclaimed.

"Did the Indians make war whoops and carry tomahawks?" Freddie asked excitedly.

"I'm afraid they did," Mr. Wheeler answered. "It was a fierce attack, and so far as any of the nearby settlers could find out, there was only one known survivor—Mary Lou, who was found wandering in the woods by the settlers."

Tears came to Flossie's eyes. "Then she had no mother or father any more?" the little girl asked.

"No," Mr. Wheeler said. "Mary Lou was reared by the people who found her."

"What happened to her brother Douglas?" asked Freddie.

"Nobody ever found out."

The elderly man then noticed that the Bobbsey twins all looked very sad. He quickly assured them that Mary Lou Wheeler did have a happy life. She had grown up and had children of her own. "She was my grandmother, remember?" Mr. Wheeler said, smiling.

"Boy! What a story!" Bert burst out.

"But wait until you hear the rest," Mr. Wheeler continued, "about the mystery that's never been solved." He said that Mary Lou, when found, was clutching a piece of cedar bark in her chubby hands. On it was a mysterious message.

"What was it?" Nan asked eagerly.

Mr. Wheeler explained that on the smooth side of the bark were carved the words, "Little trees, big meadow." And over them was a circle of thirteen dots.

"Here, I have a photograph of it," he said.

Then he chuckled. "Instead of carrying the piece of bark around, it's much easier to carry the picture, so I can show it to people when I tell the story."

He took out his wallet, reached into it and produced a picture of the bark. The twins could see plainly the thirteen crude dots and the strange words.

"Now the mystery is," Mr. Wheeler continued, "what does this message mean?"

"Do you think it might have something to do with Silver Creek?" Nan asked.

"It could. If I go there some day, perhaps I'll find out. My grandmother herself did not know the answer to the riddle."

"Maybe we can solve the mystery for you," Bert suggested hopefully.

Mr. Wheeler smiled. "Why don't you try? I'll let you have this picture as a clue. Be careful of it, because it's the only one I have left and the negative is lost. You can send the print to me at my home." He gave the twins his address in San Francisco.

The Californian said he had always hoped that the circle of dots on the cedar bark might lead him to other members of his grandmother's family who might possibly have escaped the Indian attack. "Somehow I keep thinking that maybe one or more managed to get away alive.

But Grandmother, who moved away from here when she was eighteen, once said she was sure she was the only one left in her family."

"We'll do our best for you," Nan promised.

As Bert carefully put the picture into his pocket, Mr. Wheeler said good-by, explaining that he was leaving the plane at the next stop. The children returned to their seats. Mr. and Mrs. Bobbsey came back a moment later and heard the story. Bert showed them the picture.

Mr. Bobbsey chuckled. "Well, this trip is growing more mysterious all the time."

As the plane flew on, the family discussed the mystery of Mary Lou Wheeler. Nan believed the circle of dots represented little trees in a big meadow.

"If they were trees in existence in Mary Lou's time," said Mr. Bobbsey, "they would have grown into big ones."

"That's right," Flossie spoke up, "and they might have been cut down by now."

"Yes," Freddie said with a sigh. "Nothing may be left but a lot of stumps."

Bert put the picture into his pocket again, then rose and went to the drinking fountain. As he held the paper cup under the faucet, someone bumped into him. The boy turned, to see Mr. Radkin directly alongside him.

"So sorry," the man said. "Lost my balance."

"That's all right." Bert moved so the man might get a drink.

For the next hour the children gave their attention to the scenery below. Lush green farmland changed to barren brown slopes.

Finally Nan saw an airport in the distance. At the same time the captain's voice came over the loudspeaker. "Please fasten seat belts. We are about to land at Billings."

"Wow!" Freddie blurted out. "Montana!" He glanced out the window. "But I don't see any cowboys."

"You might see some when we land," Mrs. Bobbsey told him.

As the plane circled for a landing, the Bobbseys noticed that the airport was built atop a plateau to the north of the town itself. Soon the big craft touched down lightly on the runway, taxied to the administration building, and stopped.

A stewardess came to tell the Bobbseys they might leave the plane for a little stroll because it would not take off again for twenty minutes.

"Goody! Then we can look for cowboys!" Flossie exclaimed.

As Nan rose from her seat she noticed that Mr. Radkin had already pushed toward the door and was the first to alight from the plane. He was carrying a coat and a small suitcase.

Nan was amazed. Apparently the man was getting off here!

"Bert," she said, "let's see if anyone's meeting Mr. Radkin."

The twins hurried outside. To their surprise, the man did not go toward the airport building. Instead, he walked quickly to a small red plane standing on another runway, ready to take off.

"Maybe Mr. Radkin's going to Washington in that plane!" Nan said to her brother.

When Bert did not answer, she looked at him and noticed a strange expression come over the boy's face. He was excitedly turning his pockets inside out.

"What's the matter?" Nan asked.

"Mr. Wheeler's picture! It's gone!"

"Perhaps it fell out of your pocket in the plane," his sister suggested.

Bert dashed back inside and the stewardess helped him search for the photo. It was not in sight. Bert raced out to join his twin.

"It's not there, Nan," he said. "Now I remember what probably happened!"

He told her how Mr. Radkin had jostled him at the drinking fountain. "I'll bet he took the picture from me then," Bert said hotly.

By this time Radkin had stepped inside the small red plane, and it took off down the runway.

"Boy! I'm going to find out where he's going!" said Bert.

As the twins hurried toward the terminal building they met a uniformed man with four stripes on his sleeve.

"Are you the captain of our plane?" Nan asked him.

"If it's that one over there," the captain said, smiling, and pointing to the one on which they were traveling, "the answer is yes."

Bert inquired how they could find out the destination of the small red plane that had just taken off. The captain suggested they go to the dispatcher's tower and pointed it out.

"But hurry back because we're taking off in a few minutes," the skipper said.

Bert and Nan raced up into the dispatcher's tower which overlooked the field. The man in charge told them that the red airplane owned by Mr. Radkin was going to Boise, Idaho.

"And not to Washington?" Nan said in amazement.

"No."

Again the Bobbseys were disappointed, and wondered what they should do now. As they left the tower, Nan suggested that they consult their father.

Bert agreed. "I sure hate to have to write Mr. Wheeler that his picture's gone," he said.

The children found the rest of their family inside the waiting room and quickly informed their father what had happened.

Mr. Bobbsey was dismayed. "I'll phone the police and ask to have Mr. Radkin searched when he reaches Boise. And also ask them to find out more about the man."

While Mr. Bobbsey was at a phone doing this, Bert and Nan walked over to Flossie and Freddie.

The younger twins were talking with two cowboys, and Freddie was trying on the broadbrimmed hat of one man. It covered his eyes and made the boy's ears stick out.

Bert laughed. "Cowboy Freddie!" he said. "Where's your pony?"

Before Freddie could reply, the call came to reboard the plane. Returning the hat, Freddie said good-by to the cowboys, and he and Flossie hurried off with their brother.

After the plane had taken off again, it winged higher and higher over steep mountain peaks. As they flew over a very tall range, the captain announced to the passengers that this was the Great Divide. On one side of it the waters run eastward, and drain into the Mississippi River. On the other side of the Divide the mountain streams race westward toward the Pacific Ocean.

"I guess the water has a hard time deciding which way to go," Flossie commented, and her family laughed.

As the afternoon wore on, jagged mountains with beautiful snow caps came into sight.

"These are the Cascades," Mr. Bobbsey said to the children.

Suddenly Nan said, "I think we're going lower, Bert. My ears are buzzing."

Just then a stewardess offered them all chewing gum. "This will help your ears," she said, smiling. Then the young woman added, "Look over to your left."

The Bobbseys did this. In the distance, a mountain peak towered way above its snowclad neighbors.

"I'll bet I know what that one is," Nan said. "Mount Rainier!"

The stewardess nodded and smiled. "You're very close to your destination."

Lower and lower the plane went. Now the trees in the forest were clearly visible, together with large cuts of woodland which had been made on the mountain sides. The twins' father told them that they were flying over the giant Douglas fir forests.

"Hurray!" Freddie cried. "Our forest adventure is really going to begin now, isn't it, Daddy?"

"I have a feeling," Nan said, "that it's going to be a big adventure."

Twenty minutes later the plane landed at the giant, busy airport which serves both Seattle and Tacoma. The Bobbseys said good-by to the hostesses, saying what an enjoyable trip they had had. Then the family walked down the steps that had been pushed up to the doorway, and went inside an attractive modern building to collect their baggage.

The twins and their parents had barely entered when a voice sounded over the big loudspeakers:

"Mr. Bobbsey! Paging Mr. Bobbsey! Please come to the information desk."

Mrs. Bobbsey smiled and said, "Richard, I suppose Mr. Everett is waiting for you."

They all walked rapidly through the milling crowd to the information desk. Not seeing Mr. Everett, the twins' father said to a clerk:

"I'm Mr. Bobbsey."

"Oh, yes, sir," said the clerk. "A telegram for you."

Mr. Bobbsey signed for it, then quickly tore open the envelope. A look of alarm came over his face.

"Goodness, Richard. What's the matter?" Mrs. Bobbsey cried out.

"Is something wrong, Dad?" Bert asked.

Mr. Bobbsey's jaw grew tight. "Listen to what it says." He exhaled a deep breath.

A chill of apprehension gripped the family as their father read:

"YOUR LUMBERYARD BURNED DOWN. TOTAL LOSS. BETTER RETURN AT ONCE. (SIGNED) SAM JOHNSON."

CHAPTER X

MR. BUTTONS

THE shocking telegram caused Flossie to burst into tears. The lips of the other twins quivered. Mr. and Mrs. Bobbsey stood in stunned silence for a moment, then Mrs. Bobbsey exclaimed:

"Our—lumberyard—burned to the ground!" She grasped her husband's arm. "Oh, Richard!"

As Bert recovered from the shock he wondered if their mysterious enemy might have had something to do with the fire.

"Well," Mr. Bobbsey said bravely, "it's too bad. I only hope no one was hurt in the blaze."

Nan took her father's hand and told him how sorry she was. "I guess we'll have to go right back, won't we?"

"Yes, but first I'll telephone to see what's being done."

He hurried to a booth, his family trailing after him. They watched sadly as their father placed the call to Lakeport. All they could hear was, "What? Really? It's unthinkable!"

Finally Mr. Bobbsey came from the booth. His face was stern. "I don't know whether to be angry or relieved," he said. "This telegram is a fake! The whole thing is a big hoax!"

"You mean there was no fire?" Nan asked unbelievingly.

"None at all!" her father replied.

"Goody!" cried Flossie, and Freddie yelled, "Hurray!"

Relief shone on everyone's face, but Bert said, "That's the meanest trick anyone ever played on us! I wonder if Mr. Radkin did it."

"Possibly," said Mrs. Bobbsey, "or it could even have been that Mr. Taylor who called and said you'd be sorry if you didn't sell the property, Dick."

"Whoever it was," her husband remarked, "he's trying hard to ruin our trip."

At this moment the Bobbseys' attention was diverted to a husky, smiling man who was walking toward them. He wore blue jeans, a blue denim shirt open at the neck, and a well-worn fedora hat. His light blue eyes twinkled as he stepped up to the group.

"Mr. Bobbsey?" he asked.

"That's right."

"I'm Ole Olson, a logger from Mr. Everett's crew. He asked me to meet you."

After introductions were made, Mrs. Bobbsey asked, "How did you recognize my husband?"

"I didn't, exactly, ma'am," Mr. Olson said. "Your two sets of twins was the trademark I was looking for."

The Bobbseys laughed as the lumberman beckoned them to follow him to the baggage counter.

On the way Freddie spoke up. "Are you a real logger, Mr. Olson?"

"Yep, I'm that all right. But why don't you all call me Buttons? Everyone else does."

"I'll call you Mr. Buttons if you want me to," Flossie spoke up.

At this moment Nan noticed that the three top buttons of the man's shirt were missing. She wondered if this had anything to do with his nickname. But she said nothing.

The Bobbseys' luggage was carried to a waiting car parked outside the terminal building.

"Look! It's a bus!" Flossie exclaimed, skipping over to the long vehicle into which Buttons began to place the baggage.

"I guess you could call it a bus," the logger

said, "but it's really an over-sized station wagon."

Bert quickly counted the seats. "Holds twelve."

"That's right," Buttons answered, as the Bobbseys got in. "We use it to carry our crew in and out of the woods."

Nan and Bert slipped in beside the driver while Mr. and Mrs. Bobbsey and Flossie took the seats directly behind. Freddie crawled back into the last seat with the bags.

As Buttons drove along the highway, Freddie called from the rear, "Why do they call you Buttons, Mr. Olson?"

The man chuckled. "When I was a young fellow doing some logging in Alaska," he said, "I came face to face with a bear."

"Oh!" Flossie said, "was he friendly?"

"Not this one. He took a swipe at me, but I jumped back just in time. The bear's paw, however, did rip off the top three buttons on my shirt."

The lumberman said that he turned and fled from the bear and was fortunate to escape without serious injury.

"I figured I was lucky," the logger went on, "so ever since that time I have always cut the top three buttons off every work shirt I buy, just to keep my luck."

"And were you lucky ever afterward?" Flossie asked him.

"I was until recently," he replied. "But now no one seems to be having much luck in our gyppo operation. Mr. Everett tells me that you're going to solve the mystery connected with it."

"We hope to," Mr. Bobbsey answered.

As they whizzed along Buttons explained that he was the high climber of the operation and the bucker as well.

"That's great!" said Bert. "I want to see you at work."

"Freddie's a high climber too," Nan said and told about her brother's rescue by the Lakeport fire department.

"Practice a lot and you'll become a climber some day," Buttons said, laughing. "That's the only way you'll learn to get down once you're up. Well," he remarked a moment later, "we're nearly to Mr. Everett's place."

He pointed to a sign along the road. It bore the word *Puyallup* and an arrow pointing to the left.

"Pony Gallop," Flossie read it. "Is that the name of a town, Mr. Buttons?"

Buttons smiled and said, "Flossie, you came as close to pronouncing the name right as any other visitors from the east." He told the Bobbseys that *Puy* was pronounced like *pew*—as a church pew.

The twins said Puyallup over and over, and Nan guessed that it was an Indian name.

"Correct," Buttons said.

He turned into a long driveway which led through broad, flat lawns, then up a knoll to a pretty farmhouse. Buttons blew the horn, and a man and woman hurried out.

"Hello, Cliff!" Mr. Bobbsey said enthusiastically, as he stepped from the car to shake hands with a tall, slender man wearing a black mustache.

"Good to see you, Dick! And all your family. I'd like you to meet my wife."

Buttons called good-by and drove off. The Bobbseys turned to meet Mrs. Everett, who was a short, plump woman. She greeted the Bobbseys with a hospitable smile, and they followed her inside. After hearing about their trip and the worrisome telegram, she said:

"We've had some more bad luck too. Did Buttons tell you about our dog?"

"No," Bert replied.

Mrs. Everett said that Buster, their spaniel watchdog, had been stolen the night before.

"At least," Mr. Everett spoke up, "we think he was stolen. Buster was trained never to go off our property."

"Oh, how sad!" Nan said sympathetically. "I do hope he gets away and comes back."

Mrs. Everett showed the Bobbseys to their three bedrooms on the second floor.

"Our children are grown now and have moved away, so we have plenty of room," she said.

The clean, fresh smell of the mountain air made Freddie feel energetic. After unpacking his small suitcase he turned to Bert, who shared the same room.

"Let's go outdoors and explore," Freddie suggested.

"Okay. I saw a big barn in the back. I wonder what's in it."

As they passed Nan and Flossie's room the girls wanted to know where the boys were heading. "I want to go too," said Flossie.

Nan came along, and was glad it was still light enough for them to look about the grounds. Bert and Nan went into the barn, which was filled with farming machinery and tools.

Freddie and Flossie walked into a field behind the barn. The sunset's afterglow cast a reddish light on something moving in the middle of the field.

"Look! A deer!" Flossie said, pointing.

The beautiful buck held its head erect, the antlers standing out clearly.

"Let's see if we can pat it," Freddie suggested.

Holding hands, the twins slowly approached the deer. The animal stood still until Freddie and Flossie were quite close. Then it turned and bounded across the field with graceful leaps.

"Maybe we can catch him," Freddie said and ran after the lovely creature.

Presently the deer reached the highway and stood quietly on the shoulder of the road. As the Bobbseys approached the animal, he stepped onto the road.

Just then a truck pulling a large flat trailer roared along the highway. The children were frightened. The deer seemed to have frozen—he might be hit!

"Get out of the way! Quick! Run!" Freddie shouted.

"Please jump!" Flossie begged as the truck headed directly for the deer without slackening speed.

Flossie covered her eyes. Then when the truck was only a few feet from the frightened buck, he leaped across the road and disappeared into a thicket.

As the truck whizzed past, Freddie noticed that the driver was a sour-looking man with a flat nose. On the trailer behind him was a caterpillar tractor with the name *Peggy* painted on the side of it.

"That mean driver!" Flossie said, opening her eyes.

She was thankful the buck was safe and ran to the barn to tell Bert and Nan what they had seen.

Mr. Everett was there. "I'm glad the old buck got away," he said. "Say, maybe we can catch a baby deer before you leave." The lumberman explained that fawns were born during the first ten days of June.

"You mean all baby deer have birthdays at once?" Flossie asked.

Mr. Everett said that this was nature's way of doing things. "Baby deer can't run fast when less than twenty-four hours old. That's when we might get one. But on the second day of his life he'd be too fast to be caught."

After supper the conversation turned to the mysterious goings-on in the gyppo organization. Both Mr. Bobbsey and his partner stood firm on their business agreement: They would not sell to anybody!

"I think whoever is behind this is trying to force us to give up," Mr. Everett said. He told of thefts of more equipment that had taken place recently on the job.

Suddenly Bert asked, "Do you lock your barn at night?"

"We never have," Mr. Everett replied. "People have always been honest hereabouts. Besides, we had Buster to look after things."

Mrs. Everett said it would be a good idea to get a lock for the barn the next day.

"I'll have Buttons put one on," her husband agreed.

The Bobbsey twins went to bed tired but happy. Soon they were fast asleep.

In the middle of the night Bert awakened suddenly. As his eyes opened, he looked about the room. At first the boy did not know where he was, and it took him several seconds to realize that he was not at home in Lakeport. Then he heard the sound of steps outside.

"I guess that's what awakened me," Bert told himself.

He stepped out of bed and looked through the open window. A man was moving stealthily toward the barn door!

Bert's heart pounded with excitement. "Stop!" he shouted. "Stop!"

Suddenly the prowler clicked on a powerful flashlight and turned the beam directly into Bert's face!

CHAPTER XI

AN INDIAN FRIEND

THE glare of the prowler's flashlight blinded Bert momentarily. But again he shouted:

"Stop, whoever you are!"

Instead, the man flicked off his light and darted along the shadows toward the driveway.

By now Bert's cries had aroused the others in the farmhouse. Having seen the light outdoors, Mr. Bobbsey and Mr. Everett had thrown on their robes and slippers and run downstairs. Mr. Bobbsey, in the lead, saw the prowler far up the drive and raced after him. The blurred figure paused for a moment, dropped something, then dashed full tilt toward the road.

From the second floor Bert saw him hop into a waiting car and disappear. The boy grabbed a flashlight, raced downstairs, and joined the men.

"Look at this!" Mr. Bobbsey cried, bending over.

Bert flashed his light down. In the beam lay a chain saw of the sort used by the lumbermen.

"My saw! A thief was taking it!" Mr. Everett cried out. "Those troublemakers are getting bolder." After a moment he added, "But thanks to you, Bert, that thief didn't get away with it this time."

"Did you see what the man looked like, son?" Mr. Bobbsey asked.

Disappointed, Bert said no, he had not been able to, because of the light shining in his eyes.

He helped Mr. Everett pick up the saw and carry it back to the barn.

"I certainly miss our dog Buster," Mr. Everett remarked. "I think I'd better stay out here for the rest of the night. And in the morning I'll report the prowler to the police."

Next morning after breakfast the twins looked about for any clues which the prowler might have left, but found nothing. Buttons, in the meantime, was putting a strong lock on the barn door.

When he finished, the logger called out, "Who wants to see a gyppo operation?"

"I know we all do," Nan said, laughing.

Before leaving, Mr. Bobbsey announced he had learned that Mr. Radkin's plane had never landed in Boise. "The authorities have no record of where it came down," he said.

All six Bobbseys and Mr. Everett set off with Buttons in the large station wagon.

Presently they passed a sign reading: *Silver Creek—5 miles.* A few moments later, the station wagon rumbled across a small wooden bridge beneath which ran a narrow stream.

"Is that how the place, Silver Creek, got its name?" guessed Nan.

"Yes," replied Mr. Everett. "And Silver Creek is the name of both the site of our gyppo operation, which is within the town limits, and the town itself."

In a little while Buttons turned onto a forest road. As they drove along, it rose and twisted higher into the hills. The forest on both sides became denser and the trees taller.

Buttons stopped the car and pointed up the slope of a mountain. "There's a seed block," he said.

A strip of trees stretched along a rim of the hill, while below, on the slope, the forest had been cut down.

"It looks like a crew cut," Bert remarked.

Mr. Everett explained that whenever a large section of trees was to be felled, the loggers always left a sturdy patch standing so that seeds from the pine cones would be blown by the wind and eventually reforest the area.

As Buttons started the car again, Flossie said,

"It's too bad about the forest Indians. They have no more place to live."

Buttons told her not to worry. He explained that members of the Indian tribes who used to live in the forest had married white settlers many years before.

"However, there are a few pure-blooded Indians left," he said. "Flossie, would you like to meet a little Indian girl?"

"Oh, yes!" Flossie answered excitedly.

Buttons said that a girl named Honey Littlefoot lived near by. She and her mother, Mrs. May Littlefoot, ran a refreshment and souvenir stand a mile up the road.

Nan smiled. "I'd like to meet the little Indian girl and her mother too."

"And get a bottle of soda pop from them," Freddie chimed in.

Minutes later they stopped in front of the rustic roadside stand. Mrs. Littlefoot was grilling frankfurters while her daughter Honey served a man seated in one of the small booths.

The Indian woman wore her dark hair in braids over her shoulders. She had lively brown eyes and smiled at the visitors when introduced by Buttons. "I am happy to meet people from the East," she said.

Then she called her daughter to meet the Bobbsey twins. Honey, who was eight years old, looked much like her mother except that her black hair was pulled back into a tiny pony tail.

Honey, Flossie, and Nan began to chat gaily, while the two boys selected the kind of soda they wanted. Bert reached into a self-service cooler and pulled out a bottle of sarsaparilla for himself and lemon for Freddie.

"I'll have a peach ice-cream cone, please," Flossie told Honey.

"And one for me," Nan added.

As the boys tilted the bottles up to their lips, they looked at the pictures on postcards in a rack. When Freddie finished his drink, the little boy, without thinking what he was doing, poked a finger into the neck of the bottle. Realizing this, he swung the bottle back and forth to free his finger.

Suddenly he exclaimed, "Bert, it won't come off!"

"What?"

"The bottle. It's stuck!"

At first Bert thought that Freddie was fooling. He himself had worried his mother once by doing the same trick.

But the younger Bobbsey boy was in earnest. He pulled and tugged at the bottle. It would not slide off his finger.

"Help me, Bert," Freddie begged.

Bert grabbed the bottle and pulled hard. It

would not budge. "Hold on to that wooden post by the booth," Bert directed, "and I'll pull harder."

All the other children came to watch. Freddie hooked one arm about the post, and Bert yanked on the bottle. Suddenly there was a *plop!* and Freddie's finger was released. But Bert lost his balance and teetered backward, the bottle in his hand.

A helpless look came over the boy's face as he tried vainly to regain his footing. Back went Bert on his heels until he fell into one of the booths against the man seated inside. The man lurched forward, nearly putting his nose into the custard pie he was eating.

"Hey, what's going on here!" he cried out in a startled voice.

As Freddie saw his face, his mouth formed a perfect O, and his eyes widened. "You're the man who nearly hit that poor deer yesterday!" he accused him.

The commotion and the conversation attracted the grownups and the girls. They hurried to the spot as Bert apologized for bumping into the stranger, whose nose was so flat he could be easily recognized.

Flossie asked him, "Don't you like deer?"

The man looked embarrassed. "I don't know what you kids are talking about," he said.

When questioned by Bert and Nan, he denied being the one who had driven the truck the evening before. "You must have me mixed up with someone else," the man said.

He finished his pie in two gulps, drained his cup of coffee and hurried off.

"He *is* the one, I know he is," Freddie insisted. "Mr. Flatnose is just a big old fibber."

Mrs. Bobbsey quieted Freddie while Nan said to Honey, "Have you ever seen that man before?"

The Indian girl said yes. The man had been in the shop the day before. Although he was driving a car today, he had had an empty trailer truck on his previous visit.

"And you know something funny?" Honey went on. "Yesterday he asked us for some empty milk bottles and took them with him."

Bert scratched his head and remarked, "I wonder what he wanted those for?" No one could guess why.

By this time the twins had finished their refreshments. The Bobbseys and Mr. Everett climbed into the station wagon. They waved good-by to the Littlefoots, and Buttons drove away deeper into the forest. Finally he turned into a private road, from which the pleasing aroma of fir and pine filled the air.

"This is the Bobbsey-Everett property," Mr. Everett explained.

"Oh, it's bee-yoo-ti-ful!" Flossie said, and the others agreed.

The car crossed a bridge under which churned a foaming stream. As they drove along, Mr. Everett explained that the trees were grown as a crop.

"We look sixty years ahead to the next cutting," he remarked.

Flossie thought it would be nicer to raise vegetables and flowers which they could pick in their garden every year.

"Besides," Bert said, his eyes twinkling, "how would we get anything to eat if we had to wait sixty years?"

Mr. Everett smiled and asked if the children knew that one giant fir tree was all the lumber that was needed to build a big house.

The older twins were amazed to hear this. Even Freddie was impressed, although he smiled to himself. He knew that only one small apple tree was all he needed for a tree house!

Just then a car came speeding toward them around a curve in the road ahead. With screeching brakes, the oncoming automobile stopped. Buttons pulled up beside the driver, a young fellow who had an agitated look. Mr. Everett told the Bobbseys he was Chris Johnson, a "faller" in his logging crew.

"Chris cuts down trees," he explained, introducing him.

"What's the matter, Chris?" Buttons called out. "You look as though a grizzly were chasing you."

"It's worse than that, Buttons," the young man responded. "More bad news."

CHAPTER XII

THE DONKEY DOCTOR

"OUR caterpillar tractor is gone!" Chris said worriedly. "Stolen!"

The others groaned as he explained that when they stopped work the day before, the workmen had driven the machine into a thicket. Then they had camouflaged the spot just in case some thief should come prowling around.

"But when we got ready to use the tractor this morning," Chris said, "we found it had disappeared. Now we can't pull the logs up to the truck for loading."

"Don't worry too much about that," Buttons said. "I intended to use a high line today anyhow. The slope is almost too steep for the tractor."

Bert's mind was working fast. "Couldn't you follow the tread marks of the tractor?"

Chris said that the machine apparently had

been loaded onto a flat trailer before being carted off.

"We tried to distinguish the truck's tire marks but couldn't make them out," he explained. "I sure hate to lose *Peggy*. That's the pet name of our tractor," he told the Bobbseys.

"*Peggy?* Tractor?" Freddie repeated. His eyes sparkled as he said, "I know about that!"

"What!" Chris asked.

Freddie said importantly, "I saw *Peggy* getting a ride on a trailer."

"When?"

"Where?"

Questions flew so fast that at first Freddie had no chance to answer. "It was when Flossie and I were chasing the deer yesterday just at sundown," he managed to say finally, and told about seeing the truck and trailer driven by the man whom Freddie had nicknamed Mr. Flatnose.

"You mean the one we just saw at May Littlefoot's place?" Mr. Bobbsey asked.

"Yes, Dad," Freddie said.

The men were grateful for the clue, but they feared that the missing caterpillar tractor was many miles away by now. "It'll be hard to trace," Chris remarked.

Bert and Nan were not so sure of this. "If Mr. Flatnose is still near by," Nan said, "maybe *Peggy* is too."

"I think the police should know about the theft right away," Mr. Bobbsey said.

The camp wagon was equipped with a two-way radio. Soon the police were being notified to look for *Peggy* and a man with a flat nose.

Then Chris turned his car around carefully in the narrow road and followed the camp wagon up the hill to a clearing. Here three men were loading logs onto a truck by means of a small engine with a steel cable.

When the Bobbseys got out of the station wagon with Buttons and Mr. Everett, the men stopped their work and came forward. One of them, a tall, broad-shouldered fellow, was introduced as Bill Hart, another faller.

Tony Corelli was the next to shake hands. He was a shorter, stocky man with flashing dark eyes and a broad smile.

"Tony's our catskinner." Buttons grinned, looking straight at Flossie.

"Oh, I know what a catskinner is," the little girl said. "He doesn't skin cats." Everyone laughed.

The last man to be introduced was Amos Bergen. He was red-headed, tall, and lanky.

"Amos is our donkey doctor," Mr. Everett said.

Instinctively the Bobbsey twins glanced about the clearing.

"Oh, I know you don't see any donkeys," Mr. Everett said, chuckling. "Not real live ones, anyhow."

The lumberman explained that the donkey to which he referred was the engine which supplied power to lift the logs.

"And a donkey doctor," he went on, "is a man who knows all about a donkey engine."

With the introductions over, talk turned to the theft of *Peggy*. Bert took Nan aside.

"Let's search for clues," he proposed.

The twins gazed at the ground adjacent to the spot from which the tractor had been stolen. They could see nothing but the heavy tread marks left by *Peggy* in the spongy ground covered with pine needles. Bert and Nan followed the marks until they ended about fifty feet away.

"This is where the tractor was hauled aboard the trailer," Bert remarked.

His sister was about to sit down on a freshly cut stump in order to think harder about the mystery when suddenly she cried out, "Bert!"

Bert hurried over. Nan pointed to the side of the stump, then picked up a piece of dark blue cloth. It was the right half of the front section of a man's work shirt. The three top buttons were missing!

Nan looked at Bert. "This clue points directly to Buttons, doesn't it?"

Her brother had to agree. "But I don't understand it, Nan. Why would he leave the piece here?"

His sister shrugged but decided to speak to him. The men had started working again, and Buttons was helping load logs onto the truck.

As Nan walked up, she remarked, "That's a nice new shirt you have on today."

The logger grinned and stopped to mop his brow. "I suppose you're wondering if I snipped the first three buttons off. Well, my wife did that at home yesterday. She saves them in her button box just in case I lose another button."

Bert and Nan were sure he was telling the truth but decided to speak to their mother about it. They walked to the other side of the truck where Mr. and Mrs. Bobbsey were watching the loading operation.

"Do you think Buttons came here last night after the others left?" Nan asked, showing Mrs. Bobbsey the piece of blue shirt.

"Oh, I hardly think such a nice man could be suspected," said the twins' mother.

She thought they should not mention it further at this moment but keep on the lookout for more clues.

"Let's have Flossie and Freddie help us," Nan suggested and called the small twins. "How would you like to hunt for clues?"

"Oh, yes," they chorused.

Freddie teamed up with Bert, and Nan with Flossie. As the donkey engine chugged and the cables strained to lift the logs onto the truck, the four children moved about the area as if looking for something they had lost.

While sleuthing, Bert's thoughts went back to the intruder who had tried to steal the chain-saw from Mr. Everett. Did the man Freddie called Mr. Flatnose have anything to do with it, the boy wondered. Meanwhile, the girls had found some footprints near the spot where the tractor had stood.

"They look like awfully large feet," Flossie said, bending down to examine the prints. "Do you suppose they were made by a bear, Nan?"

Her sister chuckled, saying that the imprint was made by a man's shoe. "Flossie, you know bears go *bare*foot."

Flossie giggled at the joke, then said, "Oh, look, Nan! The footprints lead over here."

Both girls followed them cautiously, bending down to examine the soft ground. The prints ended near the truck which was being loaded.

Suddenly Bert's voice rang out. "Nan! Flossie! Watch out!"

The girls glanced up just in time to see the top log on the truck fall over the side. Nan grabbed Flossie's hand, and together

"Nan! Flossie! Watch out!" Bert cried

both girls jumped out of the way just in time.

Bangedy bang! The log fell to the ground and rolled over to the spot where they had stood only a moment before. Instantly the workmen stopped what they were doing and rushed to see if the two girls had been hurt.

"We're all right," Nan assured them.

"Please don't ever play near a truck which is being loaded," Amos Bergen warned them. The girls promised to be more careful.

The donkey doctor quickly fixed a cable onto the fallen log and lifted it to the top of the truck. Then, with his engine chugging and the wheels rumbling, Tony drove off to the mill.

Nan and Flossie showed the others the big footprints. At once, Mr. Bobbsey said, "From the length of the print I judge that the shoe is about size 14."

"No one in our crew," Buttons spoke up, "has feet as large as that. They must belong to the thief. We'll tell the police about it," and the new clue was given over the radio.

Buttons said that the crew would now cut more trees. The twins gathered near the next one to be felled. With a buzzing power saw Bill Hart and Buttons cut deeply into the Douglas fir near its base. About halfway through, they withdrew the saw and carried it to the opposite side of the tree to start a cut there.

all the poor animals that would be killed," she said. "Not to mention all the wonderful trees."

"If Mr. Flatnose did want to set a forest fire," Bert remarked, "it could be for only one reason. That would be to put Dad's gyppo outfit out of business."

Buttons nodded. He spoke of the danger of forest fires, and said that the lumbermen did not like to work on days with low humidity.

"I should think they'd like to, because then the air is dry," Bert remarked. "Wouldn't it be more comfortable?"

"More comfortable perhaps," Buttons agreed, "but a lot more chance of fires."

He reminded them of how many fires were caused by friction. Once, the year before, a cable, dragging over a log, threw off sparks which started a fire.

"So the men would much rather work in the rain," Bill spoke up. "It's safer."

When the loggers returned to their work, the twins continued to play on the hillside. Flossie finally found a stump which was low enough for her to climb up and look down.

To her surprise, the little girl noticed a piece of white paper sticking out of a hole on the side of the stump. She pulled it out.

"Nan, come over here!" she called.

Her sister ran up, and together they laid the

piece of paper flat on top of the trunk. It was a note, in what seemed to be a child's handwriting, asking the logger who found it to be on the lookout for her papoose. The message was signed with a sketch of a little foot. Bert and Freddie had come over to see the note.

"I'll bet I know who wrote it!" Flossie laughed. "Honey Littlefoot!"

"She's not old enough to have a papoose," Freddie said. "It must be somebody else."

Bert had an idea. "Do you suppose it's a papoose doll Honey is looking for?"

"That's right," Freddie agreed. "You're smart, Bert."

The twins began to look for a papoose doll. As they hunted, Nan surmised that Honey must have come here for a picnic and had lost her doll while playing with it on the hillside.

Presently Freddie saw something that he thought was very peculiar and might be a clue. A tiny hand reached up from beneath a pile of wood chips. Freddie tugged at the little hand, and out came a papoose doll.

"Hurray! Hurray! I've found it!" he yelled, holding the doll up and prancing about wildly.

His two sisters crowded around and examined the doll. It was a little damp from lying in the slash, but Nan thought that if they laid the toy papoose on a stump it would dry out quickly.

Flossie fondled the cute little doll. "Oh, I just can't wait to see Honey Littlefoot and return you to her," she said excitedly.

Just then a call came from Buttons. He asked the twins if they would like to see a high line rigged up.

"You bet," said Bert.

Flossie placed the doll on a stump to dry, then the children hurried up the hill.

Buttons had selected a tall tree. He stood beside it, wearing spikes on his shoes, a stout belt, and carried an axe.

"This tree will be our spar," he said. "Now watch what I do." He started up the tree, cutting off limbs overhead as he went.

Up, up, and up he climbed. The Bobbseys tilted their heads back and kept their eyes on the high climber. Finally, from near the top of the tree, Buttons called down:

"I'm going to top her!"

Mr. Everett ordered the Bobbseys to stand back a safe distance while Buttons whacked at the tree trunk. Presently the top section keeled over and came crashing to the ground.

"Oh, look! Now it's a telephone pole!" Freddie remarked. Then he and the others began to laugh as Buttons did a little jig. Then he fastened a pulley to the tree.

With the assistance of the other lumbermen,

he now attached guy wires from adjoining trees to the top of the pole. Bill, standing near the Bobbseys, explained to them that this was to steady the spar tree.

Next, a long cable was unwound from a drum on the donkey engine, pulled up through the pulley, and extended far down the steep hillside.

As they watched the operation, Bert and Nan figured out what was going to happen. The trees on the slope would be dragged by the stout cable to a spot where they could be loaded onto the truck.

"And now," Buttons said after he had climbed down from the tree, "how would you Bobbseys like to help in this high-line logging?"

"I sure would."

"Swell."

"Tell us how."

The children crowded around, eager to try their hand at lumbering.

"We'll need a whistle punk," Buttons remarked.

"Whizzikers! What's that?" Freddie asked.

"Well, come with me and I'll show you," Buttons said as the other workmen smiled.

They followed him down the hillside to a spot where several big trees had been felled and cut into proper lengths.

"Now," Buttons asked, "can you see the donkey doctor from here?"

The Bobbseys craned their necks, but they were so far down the hillside that they could not see Amos Bergen operating the engine.

"That's where the whistle punk comes in," Buttons explained. He reached a hand into his pocket and pulled out a small whistle. "This'll be used for a code signal to Amos," he explained. "One toot will mean to lower the cable. Two toots will mean pull it up."

Bert and Nan thought that the younger twins should be whistle punks first. Flossie took the whistle in her hand.

Buttons attached the cable to the big log. Flossie gave two toots and up it went, high above their heads and over the top of the ridge.

"It's my turn now," Freddie said.

The cable was returned, but this time not far enough. Freddie gave one toot. The cable came lower and Buttons grabbed it. Then after the cable had been secured about the log, Freddie gave two toots and up went the second log.

Bert and Nan played whistle punk too, and soon all the lengths of timber had been lifted from the side of the hill. As the sun sank lower in the west, the children climbed to the top of the ridge. They found their mother there scanning the countryside with binoculars.

"Look here, children," she called. "I have a surprise for you."

Freddie reached her first and took the binoculars. Focusing on the other slope, where his mother had pointed, he saw a bear and her three cubs eating berries.

Flossie looked next. "Oh, aren't they cunning!" she said. "I love bears!"

Nan took the binoculars and watched the animals for more than a minute. The frisky little cubs rolled about, while the mother stood by, casting a wary eye over the countryside.

When it was Bert's turn, he could not find the spot at first. His eyes roved around the opposite mountain. Suddenly he cried out in astonishment:

"Someone's spying on us!"

"Can you tell who he is?" Nan asked.

"No, his face is hidden by leaves."

Hearing the conversation, Mr. Everett reached for the glasses.

"Look in that tall tree on the top of the rise," Bert directed.

Mr. Everett said he could see the person plainly. A man sat in the topmost branches, taking in the gyppo operation.

"Maybe he's Flatnose!" Nan exclaimed.

Mr. Everett suddenly said, "Oh, I can see his face now! It's thin and—you look."

Bert grabbed the glasses, but as he spotted the watcher, the fellow hid his face again. Then, nimble as a monkey, he climbed down the tree and disappeared.

"Oh, I wish I'd seen him," Bert fumed.

"Maybe it was Mr. Radkin!" Nan suggested. "Mr. Everett, did this man have big ears?"

"Why, yes, he did."

"Then I'm sure it was Mr. Radkin. He came *here* in his plane instead of going to Idaho!"

"I wish we could find out," Mr. Bobbsey spoke up. "But this is a vast territory in which to locate anyone."

"We'll just have to keep our eyes open," his partner remarked. "And now, I think we'd better leave for home."

Nan and Flossie ran to get the papoose doll from the stump. It had thoroughly dried out. The girls were the last ones to climb into the station wagon. A little later they pulled up in front of the Littlefoots' roadside stand. Honey ran out to greet them. Flossie held the papoose doll toward her.

The little Indian girl nearly burst into tears when she saw it. "Oh, Nagoma!" she cried, and hugged her dolly. "Where did you find my Nagoma?" she asked the Bobbseys.

Freddie told the story, saying he had found the doll.

"You've made me so happy," said Honey. "I wish I could do something for you."

"Maybe you can," Bert said, smiling. "Has Mr. Flatnose returned yet?"

Neither Honey nor her mother had seen the odd-looking fellow, but promised to keep on the lookout for him.

Nan had thought of another way the Indians might help the Bobbseys. By some remote chance the Littlefoots might know something about the mystery of the little pioneer girl, Mary Lou Wheeler, and the circle of dots and message on the cedar bark.

She asked May Littlefoot this question. The Indian woman thought for a long time. Finally she said:

"I myself know nothing of such a mystery. But perhaps my father would. He has heard many, many strange stories in his life. He is an old man now, the last chief of our tribe."

The twins were excited. If they could only talk with the Indian chief!

Honey, looking very proud, said, "My grandfather, Chief Lightfeather, is coming to visit us tomorrow."

"Yes," Mrs. Littlefoot said. Smiling, she asked the twins, "Would you like to meet him?"

CHAPTER XIV

THE WAR DANCE

"WE'RE going to meet an Indian chief! Hurray!" shouted Freddie from the rear of the big station wagon.

All the twins were overjoyed. Perhaps May Lightfoot's father would have the answer to the riddle on the cedar bark!

The Indian woman said she was amazed at the twins' sleuthing ability. "I hope we can help you," she said, smiling. "Come over early tomorrow."

The Bobbseys and their friends now said good-by, and Buttons drove toward home. He was so good-natured and friendly that Bert and Nan were sure that he was in no way connected with the theft of the caterpillar tractor. They held a whispered conversation in the middle section of the station wagon.

"Let's talk to him about the piece of shirt we found on the stump," Nan suggested.

"Okay."

As soon as they reached the Everett house, the twins took Buttons aside, and Nan showed him the blue material. The logger was amazed to hear the story. Then all at once he slapped his fist into the palm of his hand.

"What detectives you are!" he shouted. "You've solved a mystery for me."

"We have?" Bert asked.

"Yes. Three days ago my wife told me that one of my blue shirts had been stolen off the clothesline. Hmmm! Looks like someone was trying to throw suspicion on me for the tractor theft."

After a pause he added, with a grim look of determination, "If I ever catch the fellow who did it, I'll haul him to the top of a spar tree!"

After Buttons had left, Bert asked Mr. Everett's permission to do some phoning. First he called police headquarters to inquire about the missing tractor. He learned there was no trace of it nor of the suspect with the flat nose.

Next, Bert and Nan checked on Tacoma and Seattle hotels and motels in an effort to learn whether Mr. Radkin was in the area. After calls to ten places, Nan, whose turn it was to phone, excitedly motioned to Bert. Holding her hand over the mouthpiece, she whispered to her brother:

"There was a Mr. Radkin at this motel."

She talked with the clerk a little longer. "You heard Mr. Radkin remark that he was going to Silver Creek?" she said. "Thank you very much."

Nan hung up and turned to Bert. "Oh, I'm sure it's the same Mr. Radkin who was in Lakeport and on our plane."

"I agree," said Bert. "I'll bet he's working with Flatnose and is responsible for all the trouble to Dad and Mr. Everett."

Excitedly the children told their suspicions to the men. At once Mr. Everett phoned to several friends of his in the lumber business. He told them about the person they had seen spying on the gyppo operation and asked that they question any strangers they saw in the area.

Just before the twins went to bed, Nan said good night to Mr. Everett and remarked, "I hope that we have a good day tomorrow."

He shook his head and said, "The weather report forecasts low humidity, and that's not good for lumbering." He winked. "But it will be good for detective work!"

The following day dawned crisp and clear. The twins dressed hurriedly and ran downstairs, eager to be off to the woods again. But their faces fell when they learned that their father and Mr. Everett already had left for the forest.

"Don't be too disappointed," Mrs. Everett said kindly. "The gyppo crew was called out to work at four A.M."

"Yes," Mrs. Bobbsey added. "You children were sleeping so soundly, we didn't want to waken you."

Mrs. Everett explained that because of the low humidity the workers had gone into the woods before dawn. "They'll be able to finish their work by noon," she said, "without the danger of fire."

"Anyhow," Mrs. Bobbsey reminded the twins, smiling, "we have a date at Mrs. Littlefoot's place to meet her father."

"Yes," said Flossie. "I hope Chief Light-feather wears his feather headdress."

"And has his braves with him," Freddie added.

Mrs. Bobbsey reminded her son that the old man probably would be alone.

After breakfast Mrs. Bobbsey and the twins helped Mrs. Everett with the housework. The girls assisted in making the beds while the boys washed the breakfast dishes. When all the tasks were finished, their hostess drove the group to the Littlefoot shop.

Honey and her mother greeted them, then Mrs. Littlefoot said, "Come into our living room back of the shop. My father has arrived and is eager to meet you."

She led the way and opened the door to an attractive room furnished with bright-colored Indian rugs and pine furniture. Seated on a straight-back chair was an elderly Indian in full regalia.

"My father, Chief Lightfeather," said his daughter. "My worthy father, this is Mrs. Everett, Mrs. Bobbsey, and the Bobbsey twins."

The children bowed, and Chief Lightfeather held out his hand.

"Come here, my children," the old man said.

They all gathered around him, including Honey. Mrs. Littlefoot smiled at Mrs. Bobbsey and suggested that the three women leave the children alone with the chief. They went out, closing the door.

Chief Lightfeather put an arm around his granddaughter Honey. "I'm very proud of her," he told the Bobbseys. "She can do a very fine Indian dance."

"We'd like to see it," Nan said. "Will you dance for us, Honey?"

The little girl nodded, then went into an adjoining bedroom. In a few moments she returned, wearing a costume and carrying an Indian drum which she gave to her grandfather. Chief Lightfeather began to beat it with his fingertips, and chanted an Indian song in a high-pitched voice.

Then Honey started her Indian dance. First she swayed from left to right, making her feet keep time with the drum. After that she danced in a circle. As the music became faster, she fairly flew around the room. The old Indian grinned broadly.

"Come on," Honey said to the twins, "dance along with me."

She reached out and grasped
Flossie's hand. The little twin
tried to imitate the Indian girl.
Then Freddie joined in, and it was
not long before all the Bobbseys
were dancing about. Around in
a circle they went, stomping
louder the faster they
danced.

Finally Freddie put the flat of his hand to
his mouth and gave a couple of war whoops.
Seeing that this pleased the old chief, all the
children began yelling. There was a great din
until finally the door burst open and Mrs. Littlefoot stuck her head in.

"My goodness," she said, laughing, "you're frightening all my customers away with your war whoops."

The children promised to be more quiet, and the dance ended. Nan said, "Honey, may we ask your grandfather some questions now?"

"Yes. Go ahead."

All the children sat down cross-legged on the floor before the old Indian chief. Nan asked him if he knew the meaning of a design which was a circle of dots on a piece of cedar bark.

The old man looked up at the ceiling for a few minutes as if searching his memory. At last, he shook his head.

"The only thing I can remember about a circle of dots," Chief Lightfeather said slowly, "is that I painted such a design on one of my drums when I was a youth. I am afraid that is no help to you, however. My design had no particular meaning."

The twins, disappointed, were silent for a moment. Then Bert decided to question the chief about something else.

"Did you ever know, or hear of, a white child named Mary Lou Wheeler?" he asked.

Again Chief Lightfeather shook his head. "No." After a minute of deep thought, he continued, "But that does bring to my mind the white Indian of our tribe."

At mention of a white Indian, the twins were perplexed, but keenly interested. "Please tell us more about this man," Nan requested. "Who was he? Where did he come from?"

Chief Lightfeather said that, as he recalled the story, the white Indian, when a very young child, was given to his tribe by the Great Spirit. "My forebears believed this boy was meant to replace a brave killed on a raid of white travelers," the old man related. "He grew up to be one of the greatest men in our tribe."

Bert and Nan glanced at each other, their hearts thumping. Both had the same thought. Could this man have been Douglas, the missing brother of Mary Lou Wheeler?

"What was the white Indian's name?" Bert asked excitedly.

"He was called Fleet-in-the-Woods." The chief explained that the boy had earned this name because he had become the fastest runner in the tribe.

"What was his real name?" Nan prodded.

"I never heard," Chief Lightfeather replied. Then he said, "Fleet-in-the-Woods married an Indian girl."

"And did they have papooses?" Flossie asked.

Chief Lightfeather smiled and patted the little girl's head. "Yes. But I do not know where the descendants of Fleet-in-the-Woods live now." A sad expression crossed the Indian's face. "We have lost contact with all our people since Honey's father died," he explained. "I myself live in California. I visit only my daughter when I come here."

Bert then decided to tell the chief the complete story of Mary Lou Wheeler. When he had finished, the boy asked:

"If the circle of dots stood for trees, do you know where they might be?"

The old man put his hand to his forehead. "Many moons ago, I knew much about this region. But let me try to recall."

All was quiet again as Chief Lightfeather thought. Then he held his head high, and a gleam of remembrance came into his eyes.

"I think I can tell you where to look," he said.

The Bobbsey twins waited breathlessly to hear his answer.

CHAPTER XV

BERT, THE LOG ROLLER

"THE circle of trees," Chief Lightfeather began, "may be located on a straight line, as the crow flies, between the bend in Turtle River and the top of Mount Rainier. That was the route taken by the white pioneers."

"How exciting!" Nan exclaimed.

All the twins were thrilled to hear this wonderful clue. How they hoped they could find the spot! If only the circle of trees, or at least their stumps, were still there!

"Since Mary Lou Wheeler was found near by," Nan reasoned, "the trees and big meadow might be close to where her family was traveling."

Honey's grandfather smiled at the twins. "Well, I wish you luck in solving your mystery." He added laughingly, "Perhaps the circle of trees is where you'll find the treasure that's supposed to be hidden around here."

Freddie's eyes lighted up. "Treasure!"

Chief Lightfeather nodded, saying he had heard stories about some kind of buried treasure in the area. "But no one really believed this," he added.

The twins were intrigued nevertheless, and Freddie determined to look for the treasure anyway. Then the children told the elderly man how much they had enjoyed meeting him. After saying good-by, they went out to the shop.

"I'm glad you're through," said Honey's mother. "Come here quickly!" Then Mrs. Littlefoot laughed at the children's expressions.

"Oh, don't look as if you were going to see a ghost," she teased. "What I want you to look at has nothing to do with the mystery."

"Then what is it?" Freddie asked.

"Follow me," Honey's mother said and led them outdoors.

Standing near by were Mrs. Bobbsey and Mrs. Everett. They smiled at the twins as the Indian woman pointed to a wooded glen next to the roadstand. In the middle of it stood a beautiful brown bird.

"It's a grouse hen," Mrs. Littlefoot said in a low voice. "A ruffled grouse. I thought you'd like to see her."

"Oh, yes. May we get closer?" Nan asked.

"All right," Mrs. Littlefoot said, "but don't make any sudden motions. You might scare her away."

With Freddie and Flossie in the lead, the twins and Honey tiptoed quietly toward the soft brown bird with fluffed feathers around her neck.

"She looks kind of like a chicken, only prettier," Flossie remarked.

"She's called the chicken of the forest," Honey told her.

The hen looked this way and that, then walked slowly toward the road, bending over as if one wing were broken.

"The poor thing!" Nan said sympathetically.

Honey laughed. "She's all right. A mother grouse sometimes does that to fool people and keep them from looking for her chicks."

Flossie's eyes danced. "You mean she has babies hidden near here?"

"Yes," the Indian girl replied, and said that the grouse would lead her followers to a place far from the area where her babies were hidden. "Let's see where the hen will take us."

"I'll get my camera," Bert said, as the others started to tiptoe cautiously after the grouse.

He went to the car. By the time he returned the graceful bird had stopped in some tall grass near the roadside. The boy quickly focused his camera. *Click!*

"I got a beautiful picture, I think," he said proudly.

The grouse walked on farther and finally paused near the side of a car parked by the roadway. Bert knelt down, got his focus and shot another picture.

"Let's not follow her any more," Freddie proposed. "I want to hunt for the baby chicks."

"All right," Honey agreed.

She turned back in the direction from which they had come, and the Bobbseys followed. As she walked along, the Indian girl bent down to part the grass and weeds. Flossie did the same. But suddenly the little girl cried out, "Ouch!"

"What happened?" Nan said, running up to her.

"This bush—it—it bit me," Flossie said.

Nan looked down to see a small plant. It had a palmy leaf which was of deep green and contained spines on the underside of the leaf and stem.

"Oh, that's called a devil's club," Honey said. "I should have told you it will stick into your fingers if you don't look out."

Flossie decided to avoid the devil's club. Gingerly stepping over several of the plants, she followed Honey. Suddenly the Indian girl cocked her head.

"Oh, I hear the chicks," she said.

Now all the children gently searched the foliage.

"I see something!" Flossie whispered.

Honey bent in her direction. "Those are the baby chicks all right."

Gently Flossie picked up a tiny grouse and held it in the palm of her hand. The little bird's soft down was golden in hue. Flossie held it in a ray of sunlight while Bert took another picture.

"How cute!" said Nan.

After discovering three more grouse chicks, the Bobbseys returned them to their nesting place. The mother hen stood off at a distance making a scolding, clucking noise.

"All right, Mother Grouse," Flossie said, laughing, "we'll leave your babies alone now."

The children hurried back to where they had left the grownups, then drove off.

On the way home Mrs. Everett stopped at Silver Creek to do a little shopping.

Bert noticed a drugstore and said, "I'd like to have these films developed." He hopped out. When he returned, the boy was smiling. "They'll be ready tomorrow."

"I hope you got good pictures of the grouse and the chicks," said Nan. "If you didn't, I'll bet you'll be grouchy," she joked.

"Oh, that's terrible," Bert grimaced at his twin.

By the time the group reached the Everett farm, the gyppo crew had come back from the woods. Freddie ran up to his father to tell him about Chief Lightfeather.

Mr. Bobbsey was astounded. "You say the Chief mentioned some treasure buried in the circle of trees?"

"That's right, Daddy," Flossie chimed in. "And he told us where it's s'posed to be."

Even Mr. Everett was excited over the news. After hearing from the twins the location given by the Indian, he went at once to a closet and dug out an old map of the area. Placing the map on the dining-room table, he pointed out Turtle River and the top of Mount Rainier.

"But where is the crow?" Freddie asked. "I don't see any crow flying around."

Bert laughed and explained to his brother that the expression, "as the crow flies," which Chief Lightfeather had used, means, "in a straight line."

"Oh," Freddie said, and leaned his elbows on the table, his chubby hands cupping his chin.

Flossie, pushing forward for a better view, had tilted her chair.

"Look out, Flossie," Nan warned her, and grabbed the chair just in time to keep it from falling over.

"Well," Mr. Everett said, taking a pencil from his pocket, "here goes."

He drew a straight line between Turtle River and the summit of Mount Rainier and studied it.

"Well, I'll be a turtle skinner!" Mr. Everett exclaimed. "That line goes right through Silver Creek, Dick!"

"Wow!" cried Freddie. "Let's start digging."

"Hold on, son," his father said. "We can't dig on anyone else's property, and this line goes through many miles of land belonging to other people."

Bert was so excited he was pacing back and forth. "Dad, that treasure must be on *our* property. That's why the crooks want to put you and Mr. Everett out of business."

Nan and Flossie begged to look for the circle of trees.

"All right," their father agreed. "But not until tomorrow. There's something else planned for today."

The children were disappointed but asked what they would be doing. Mr. Bobbsey told them that Buttons had arranged a visit to a very large lumber mill for the twins. "He couldn't call it off now."

Mrs. Everett served a lunch of frankfurters and baked beans, and the twins ate hungrily. Shortly after the meal was over, Buttons appeared at the front door.

"Are you all ready to see the lumber mill?" he asked.

When the twins chorused "yes," the logger added with a smile, "Well, you'd better bring some cotton to stuff into your ears. It's a noisy place."

This time the children were going on the trip without their parents, and Mrs. Bobbsey cautioned them to be careful and do as they were told by Buttons.

"We will," they promised, and rode away.

As they neared the sprawling lumber mill, Buttons explained that each mill had a pond.

"For fishing?" Flossie asked innocently.

"Well, it's full of big wooden fish," Buttons answered, grinning, "only we call them logs."

He explained that the trucks dumped the logs into the mill pond where they could be easily mounted, selected, and separated on their way to the big saws.

"Here we are," Buttons said as they drove into a narrow road leading to the lumber mill.

Soon they came to a large wooden building covering several acres of ground. From inside could be heard a grinding sound accompanied by the whine of saw blades.

"May we see the pond first?" Freddie asked.

Buttons agreed that this would be the best place to start their tour. They drove behind the building, and there in a hollow lay a good-sized mill pond. It was filled with large, floating logs. Freddie begged to get out of the car and look around.

As the logger showed Bert and Nan the different kinds of timber being hauled in on long trucks, Freddie and Flossie held hands and walked to the edge of the pond.

"Oh, look, here's a boat," Freddie said, seeing one near them. "Do you want to take a ride with me, Flossie?"

"If you'll be careful," the little girl answered.

"Oh, we can swim," Freddie said. He steadied Flossie as she stepped into the small boat. Then he followed. Picking up an oar, he shoved the boat away from the shore.

"Let's make believe all these logs are whales," Freddie said, "and that we are on a whaling ship."

"Ship ahoy, Captain Whalebone!" cried Flossie, getting into the spirit of the game.

The twins had not gone far among the logs when Bert spied them. "Hey, come back here!" he called out.

"All right," Freddie shouted back. But as he tried to row the boat back to the shore, he found that the oars kept hitting the logs and he could not get them into the water.

"Hold on, I'll get you," Bert said. He turned to Buttons. "Do you suppose I can run across the logs?"

"I think so. Try it."

Bert stepped onto a near-by log. Then, before it rolled under his weight, he scooted to another, then another.

"Fine work!" Buttons called out. "You act like a full-fledged log roller!"

Finally Bert stepped onto the log next to the little boat. "Steady now while I get in," he said.

The boy kept his feet moving as the log

rolled, and swung his arms to keep his balance.

Freddie, eager to help, pulled on one of the oars. Unfortunately, it tilted the log.

"Oh!" cried Bert, as he tried to catch his balance.

But the log rolled over too far for him. He landed with a splash in a narrow strip of water between the log he was on and another near by.

As he bobbed to the surface he saw Buttons jumping across the logs with the speed of lightning. Reaching down, he pulled Bert quickly to the log again and told him to skip back to shore, leaping from log to log. The boy managed this without falling in again.

Buttons followed, pulling the boat behind him. As they reached the shore two other lumbermen awaited them.

"Everybody okay?" one asked.

"Oh, sure," Bert replied.

Buttons introduced the men as Mike and Pat and said they were pond men.

"How would you two like to give the kids an exhibition of log rolling while Bert dries off?" he asked them.

Mike and Pat grinned and nodded. They hopped nimbly onto a big pine log which lay about six feet from shore. They began to roll it over and over with their feet, first slowly, then faster and faster, until the log was churning the quiet water of the pond into a froth. Freddie and Flossie laughed gleefully, and Nan clapped at the excellent exhibition.

"Boy, I wish I could do that," Bert said admiringly as the men slowed the log again and jumped back to shore.

"You made a good start, Bert," Mike said. "It wouldn't take you long to become a fine log roller."

"I'll practice in Lakeport," the boy decided.

After Bert had sat in the sun for ten minutes his clothes were dry enough for the twins to continue their tour through the lumber mill.

Buttons led the twins up a long, covered ramp to the interior of the saw mill, where the thunder of the machinery caused Flossie to clap her hands over her ears. Presently the children found themselves on a catwalk, providing an excellent view of the giant saws and conveyor belts operating beneath them. The lumberman first directed their attention to a large room next to the mill pond. The room had a plate glass window through which the twins could watch. Before it sat a man operating many levers on a panel in front of him.

Inside the room, one log after another, having been lifted from the mill pond by chains, was being stripped of its bark. As the operator pushed and pulled the levers, he rotated the logs by means of steel claws. Then a jet of water blasted the brown bark off as easily as if it were the skin on a peach.

Buttons turned and directed the twins farther along the catwalk, pointing to a row of vertical saws. The Bobbseys watched as a huge log was pushed through the blades. Boards of equal width were cut at the same time. Freddie was fascinated.

"That should be called a layer-cake saw," he shouted above the din.

Buttons leaned close to Bert's ear in order to be heard. "Now I'll show you where wood pulp is made," he said.

He led them up a flight of steps to another catwalk. Here two conveyor belts ran alongside the children, waist high. The belts carried odds and ends of boards into the mouths of two machines set well below the floor level. As the pieces of wood dropped into the chipping machines, they were ground up.

Bert and Nan were fascinated. In order to get a better look at where the pieces of wood were coming from, Nan leaned over one of the conveyor belts. Instantly the machinery stopped.

"Oh, I've broken it!" she cried out, frightened.

CHAPTER XVI

THE TELLTALE PHOTO

ALL four of the Bobbsey twins looked at one another, frightened. Had one of them touched a button causing the belt of the machine to stop?

A workman named Tom noticed their worried expressions and hurried over to where Nan was standing.

"Did we do something wrong?" the girl asked anxiously.

Tom smiled and said, "The machine stops running whenever anything made of metal touches the conveyor belt."

"I *was* leaning over it," Nan confessed.

The workman chuckled and pointed at the belt. "Look here," he said. "Is this your necklace?" He reached down among some scraps of wood and held up a pretty silver chain.

"Oh dear!" Nan exclaimed. "Yes, that's mine!"

"It must have fallen off your neck," the man

said. As he gave the jewelry back to Nan, the machine started again. "Nothing broken, you see."

Andy, the chipping-machine man, explained that metal such as nails or bolts, if carried along on the conveyor belt, would severely damage the blades in the machine. That was why the safety device had been set up.

Freddie was impressed. "It works like magic, doesn't it?"

"And you're the magic man," Flossie added, smiling at Andy.

"Something like that," he replied, laughing. "An electronic detective stands guard at all times and lets us know when any metal suddenly shows up."

"An electronic detective?" Freddie asked. "Where is he?"

"Right here." Andy grinned and pointed to a metal box standing about three feet high and two feet across. He removed the front plate, and inside the twins saw a maze of wires and tubes.

"It looks," Freddie said, "like the inside of our television set."

"And this is what the electronic detective has caught," the man continued.

He pointed to a bucket standing beside the machine. In the bucket were pieces of metal which had stopped the machine at one time or another.

"Do you have any more magic tricks?" Flossie asked.

"I'm afraid not," Buttons spoke up. "Our tour is over."

"I've loved it all," said Nan.

"It's been swell," Bert added.

The Bobbseys returned with him along the catwalk until they came to the entrance of the lumber mill. Then they went out and climbed into the car. When they reached Silver Creek Bert asked Buttons to stop at the drugstore so he might pick up his pictures. He hopped out. Upon his return to the car a few minutes later, there was a broad smile on his face. Sliding in beside Nan, Bert said:

"The pictures turned out great. Look at this one of the grouse."

The photo showed the hen with one foot on the ground, the other raised. In the background was the car which had been parked there.

Nan took the picture to get a better look.

"Bert!" she exclaimed suddenly. "Isn't that someone peering around the side of the car?"

Her twin looked. "Sure enough! But it's blurred. He must have moved just as I snapped the picture. I didn't notice anyone around. What do you make of it, Buttons?" Bert asked.

The logger studied the picture for a moment as Flossie and Freddie peered over his shoulder.

"You're right," he said finally. "Someone definitely *was* hiding behind that car."

"But why would he be hiding?" Flossie asked.

"It's a good question," said Buttons. "I'd be inclined to think he was spying on you. Well, I don't see how you'd ever find out who he is."

Nan spoke up triumphantly. "Oh yes, we can, Buttons. Look at that license plate."

The identification tag stood out clearly, and Nan said, "All we have to do is check on the number. Probably the person who's hiding owns the car."

"Not necessarily, Nan," Bert reminded her. "The car might have been stolen!"

"That's right," Nan agreed. "Well, let's see the rest of the pictures."

The Bobbseys quickly glanced through the other prints, and Flossie said, "I like the baby grouse chick best of all."

The younger twins busied themselves studying the pictures at length, while Buttons started the car again.

Nan asked him to take them to the police station. "I think we should try to find out right away who owns the car," she said.

"All right." Presently Buttons pulled up in

front of police headquarters. He stayed in the car with Flossie and Freddie while Bert and Nan mounted the concrete steps, went inside, and walked up to the desk.

"We'd like to see the chief, please," Bert spoke up. "Our name is Bobbsey, and we're visiting the Everetts."

The desk sergeant ushered the Bobbseys into a side room, where the chief, a stocky man with a ruddy complexion, heard their story. The officer, whose name was McCormack, pressed a button on his desk and spoke into the intercom. "Send Joe in, please."

A few seconds later a handsome young officer entered and was introduced as Policeman Joe. He had jet black hair, a straight nose, and firm chin. Chief McCormack handed him the photograph and asked that he check the license number of the car.

Policeman Joe smiled at the twins, then ushered them out of the chief's office to a bench in the large room and asked that they wait there.

Bert whispered to his sister, "I hope we've discovered something worth while."

"If we have," Nan said, "Mrs. Littlefoot should be thanked for the clue. If she hadn't called us to see the grouse, you might never have snapped that picture."

Ten minutes later Policeman Joe returned

with a piece of paper in his hand. "I've checked the registration," he told the twins. "The car belongs to a Mr. John Berryman. Do you know him?"

Bert and Nan cried out excitedly, and Bert said, "If he's a lawyer, Mr. Everett knows him. He tried to buy some property from him. Thank you very much."

Elated, the twins rushed back to the car. When they told Buttons and the small twins what they had learned, the logger drove home as fast as he could within the speed limits.

The Everetts and the Bobbseys were standing in front of the house. Bert quickly got out of the station wagon and showed them the picture of the man who had been hiding back of the car.

"It's probably Mr. Berryman, the lawyer, or at least that's who owns the car," he said.

Mr. Everett was amazed and said he would get in touch with the man at once. "He didn't leave his address, but I have a book listing all the lawyers in this area. I'll look him up."

The lumberman hurried inside the house, while Mr. and Mrs. Bobbsey scanned the photos more closely.

"Here are the baby grice," Flossie said, pointing to a print of the chicks.

"The what?" Mrs. Bobbsey asked.

"The grice," her small daughter repeated, then added, "If one mouse plus one mouse makes two mice, then one grouse and one grouse make two grice. Isn't that right?"

Chuckling, Mrs. Bobbsey said that the English language did not always work that way. Two grouse were still called grouse.

"Anyway," Flossie said, pressing a chubby finger to the photograph, "here is the mother hen, and there are her chicks."

At this moment Mr. Everett came from the house holding a little white book in his hand. "Look, Dick," he exclaimed, "there isn't a lawyer hereabouts named Berryman. The man is an impostor! Too bad the fellow in Bert's picture didn't show up clearly enough to tell if he was Berryman."

Mr. Bobbsey felt that the police should be notified instantly. Mr. Everett agreed but thought he should take some immediate action.

"No workmen are at the gyppo camp right now. Those crooks may commit more mischief out there!"

"Like what?" Bert asked.

"Like damaging the rest of our equipment," Mr. Everett said. "For all we know, they may be trying to sabotage our high-line rigging at this moment!"

When Buttons heard this, he exclaimed worriedly. "They'd better not! That was the only spar tree in the area. If they should cut it down—"

"We'd better get out there right away to protect the place," Mr. Bobbsey suggested.

While Mrs. Everett went to phone the Silver Creek police, her husband, together with Mr. Bobbsey, Buttons, Bert, and Freddie, hopped into the car. They drove rapidly toward the gyppo operation.

"Things certainly are happening fast," Buttons said as he rounded a curve in the mountain road. "If this mystery isn't solved soon, we'll all be looking for other jobs."

He turned onto the private forest road and increased his speed. Finally they came to the clearing.

"Someone's over there!" Bert whispered. The man, whose back was turned to them, was so busy he evidently had not heard the car.

As it skidded to a halt Bert leaped out. The boy dashed pell-mell among some stumps toward the man, who was bending over a cable near the high-line rigging.

"Careful, Bert!" Buttons cried out as he raced far behind the boy.

"Stop whatever you're doing!" Bert challenged the intruder.

Startled, the fellow turned around. The lower part of his face was covered with a white handkerchief, and in his hand he held a hacksaw. The cable, Bert could clearly see, was half sawed through.

The man realized that Bert was about to spring on him. Instantly the masked fellow pointed to the ground and yelled: "Look out for the snake!"

CHAPTER XVII

TWIN DEER

THE warning about a snake slowed Bert for a moment, but he was not fooled. Remembering that there were no snakes in the area, he leaped toward the man and grabbed his arm, but the fellow pulled away and shook the boy off.

"Get away from me!" he yelled.

In turning to run, the fugitive banged into the partially cut cable. It snapped. One end flew high in the air. The other snaked along the ground, and the man's feet became entangled in it. He fell over, knocking the handkerchief mask off his face.

Flatnose!

The stranger had no chance of escaping now, for Bert's father, Mr. Everett, and Buttons flung themselves on the husky fellow.

"We've caught you at last!" Buttons cried.

Taking off his belt, he tied the man's ankles securely. Bert contributed his belt to link the prisoner's wrists behind his back.

"So!" Mr. Everett said, "you're the one who has been causing all the trouble for our logging operation!"

The prisoner muttered sullenly but said nothing.

"Who put you up to this?" Mr. Bobbsey asked. "And what's the reason for destroying our equipment?"

Flatnose, who lay on his side on the ground, did not reply but instead struggled to get loose.

"No use to try that," Buttons said. "You'll never get away from us."

Nevertheless, the prisoner continued to thrash about. Just then the distant wail of a siren sounded down the mountainside.

Freddie's eyes danced excitedly. "The police!"

In a few minutes a car screeched to a halt in the clearing. Two officers jumped out. One of them was Policeman Joe.

"We got the call from your farm, Mr. Everett," said Joe. "Good thing we came out. I see you have a prisoner."

Policeman Joe untied the man's feet and hands, and lifted Flatnose upright.

"What's your name?" Joe asked him.

"None of your business."

"We call him Flatnose," Freddie said, then told the officers how the man had nearly run down the big deer on the highway when he was stealing *Peggy*.

"The boy's got your number," Joe told the prisoner. "Suppose you tell us why you were sawing this cable."

Flatnose's sullen attitude made him look even uglier. "I'm not saying anything," he muttered.

"All right then," Joe said. "Maybe you'll talk in jail." He snapped handcuffs on the man and led him to the police car. Then he said to the other policeman, "I want to look around a bit."

Back at the Everett farm, meanwhile, Mrs. Bobbsey and her two daughters waited with Mrs. Everett for news from Silver Creek.

"Oh, I do hope there hasn't been any trouble," Mrs. Bobbsey said anxiously.

"I know what we can do till they return," Mrs. Everett said. "I should have thought of it before."

"Thought of what?" Flossie asked.

"Of going on a hunt for baby deer," she said. "In a few days now there won't be any more. How would you like to find a little fawn, Flossie?"

"Oh, I'd love to!" the little girl replied.

"So would I," Nan chimed in.

"Let's go right away," Mrs. Everett said. "It will take our minds off the suspense of waiting."

Getting the car, she drove them along a narrow road deep in the foothills of the fir forest. The girls looked to left and right for deer. Once Nan saw a doe bound off between the trees, but no fawns were following her.

After Mrs. Everett had driven several miles, they approached a bend in the road. As they rounded it the children gasped.

In the road, not more than a hundred feet ahead, stood a beautiful doe. Directly behind her were two spindly-legged fawns. The driver of a truck full of logs had paused at the side of the road to watch them.

"Luck is with us!" Mrs. Everett said as she slowly drove closer to the three animals.

The doe turned and looked at the car. Then she jumped into the heavy brush beside the road. Her two babies stood helpless, not knowing whether to follow their mother or to stay in the road.

"Hurry! Jump out of the car, girls," Mrs. Everett directed, stopping.

Nan and Flossie got out, followed by the others, and walked toward the baby deer.

"They're not more than twenty-four hours old," Mrs. Everett said in a low voice.

Flossie asked, "May we catch them?"

"Go ahead. Try."

The two little deer wandered to the side of
the road. One of them flattened itself out, holding its head close to the ground. Flossie bent
down and picked it up in her arms. How soft
and warm it was!

Just then the Everetts' station wagon came
along from the opposite direction and stopped.
When Bert and Freddie saw the fawns they
hopped out and ran over to them. Freddie began to play with one, while Bert climbed onto
the parked lumber truck to get a better view.

"Aren't they darling?" Flossie cooed, although she was having a struggle to hold the
little animal.

At first the fawn waved its legs, but the little
girl held it tightly. She could feel the frightened thumping of the tiny creature's heart.

Mrs. Everett, looking on, chuckled and said,
"I suppose we should call them the Bobbsey
Twins' Deer." When Bert made a face at this
suggestion, she added, "How about naming
them Freddie and Flossie?"

"Oh, that's lovely," said Flossie.

"You'd better let the fawns go now," Mrs.
Bobbsey said. She told the children there was
an old superstition that if a person touched a
baby fawn its mother would desert it.

"Don't worry about that," Mrs. Everett spoke

up. "It isn't true, for I have seen many fawns captured and released, and their mothers take care of them just as before."

Flossie and Freddie set the tiny animals far back from the road. The baby deer moved off awkwardly, their spindly legs hardly able to hold them up. As the children walked back to the cars, they could see the mother deer poking her head from the foliage. Then the two babies followed her back into the forest.

"Oh, I'm glad the mama deer came back for her Flossie and Freddie fawns," said Flossie, who had worried about this.

Now Freddie said to his sisters, "What do you think happened? We caught a bad man!"

"Really? Who was it?" Nan asked.

"Flatnose!"

Freddie and Bert excitedly poured out the story of the capture, as the girls and women listened in amazement. The boys had just finished, when Policeman Joe came up in the squad car. It pulled alongside the other automobiles and stopped. The group gazed at the prisoner.

"I'm glad I met you people," the officer said, "so I could tell you I'm sure this man is wanted by the police. I've seen his pictures on posters of wanted thieves. You've certainly been a great help. Well," he added, "I suppose I shan't see you Bobbseys again."

The twins were sorry to hear this, because they liked the young policeman, and Mr. Bobbsey said, "I guess not. Good luck to you! And by the way, what's your full name, Joe?"

"Joseph Fleetwood."

"Fleetwood?" Nan repeated. "*Fleetwood?*"

"That's it," Policeman Joe replied, smiling. "You seem surprised."

A wild idea was running through the girl's head. She wanted to ask him a question but feared she might be wrong. But, gathering her courage, Nan said:

"Policeman Joe, by any chance are you descended from a white Indian named Fleet-in-the-Woods?"

At Nan's question, the officer blinked in surprise. "Yes, I am," he said. "My grandfather's name was Fleet-in-the-Woods. My father shortened it to Fleetwood so it would be an American name." Then the officer asked, puzzled, "Where did you hear this?"

Now each of the twins took part in telling the story they had heard from Chief Lightfeather of how the white Indian boy had received this name. When they finished, the officer grinned and held a hand to his forehead.

"What detectives you children are!" he exclaimed.

"But wait," Bert spoke up. "There's more to the story."

He then related what they had learned from Mr. Wheeler, the man they had met on the plane. When Bert paused, Nan explained;

"You see, Policeman Joe, Mary Lou Wheeler's baby brother Douglas must have been captured by the Indians. They brought Douglas up, and he was the white Indian of Chief Lightfeather's tribe, the one who could run so fast—"

The young officer broke in, astounded. "That means my grandfather's real name was—Douglas Wheeler!" Excitedly he added, "My family always hoped this mystery would be cleared up. Now I can meet this Mr. Wheeler and learn a lot more about my family. You twins are wonderful!"

Bert remembered Mr. Wheeler's address and gave this to the officer. Policeman Joe now said he must leave and get his prisoner to the jail. He stepped into the squad car, a broad smile on his face.

Flatnose, however, still remained glum, and Nan wondered whether he would ever confess to all the things he had done.

As good-by's were exchanged, Nan said gaily, "We've solved one of our mysteries. Now I hope we can find the circle of trees where maybe a treasure is buried. Will you help us, Policeman Joe?"

"Indeed I will," he promised. "I'm not on duty tomorrow. Suppose I come to the Everett farm, and we'll make some plans."

After the policemen drove off with their prisoner, the Bobbseys started back to the Everett home, happy and hopeful. The next day they would go into the forest to hunt for treasure!

CHAPTER XVIII

A SURPRISING TREASURE

"OH, I hope it's not just a make-believe buried treasure," Flossie remarked that evening as the twins looked at a map spread out on the living-room floor.

Mr. Bobbsey and Mr. Everett studied the map carefully. "That line we talked about not only runs through Silver Creek, but right through our property!" Mr. Everett said excitedly.

"How could we get there?" the twins' father asked.

His partner said the only road leading into the place was narrow and rutted. In order to reach this particular acreage, they would have to hike through the woods a good distance.

"In that case we'd better get to bed early," Mrs. Bobbsey advised, and the twins went upstairs very soon.

Next morning, as they finished breakfast, Mrs. Everett sighed. "This was when I always used to feed our dog Buster," she said. "I certainly miss him."

"Maybe he'll come back some day," Nan remarked hopefully.

Shortly afterwards Joe arrived. Instead of wearing his uniform, he had on khaki trousers and shirt with high hiking boots which made him look more like an Indian than ever. He carried a walkie-talkie on his back.

After he heard where they had decided to hunt for the circle of trees, the officer smiled and said:

"Off we go!"

Joe and Buttons, who was going along, opened the doors of the big station wagon, and everybody got in. Mrs. Bobbsey and Mrs. Everett, like the others, were prepared for hiking. They wore jodhpurs and sport shirts. Bert and Freddie carried canteens of water, and the car was filled with digging tools.

The air of excitement sent chills up and down Nan's back as they drove along through the dense, sweet-smelling woodlands. Higher and higher the road led up a valley which lay between two ridges covered with Douglas fir.

Presently Buttons turned off to the right and followed a small, hilly road. Branches brushed

against the car, and the wheels bounced in and out of the ruts as the travelers made their way slowly up the hillside. Finally the road ended.

"Here's where we start our hike," Buttons said.

The men and boys picked up shovels, spades, and picks. Soon they were in the heart of the cool, dim forest. Only here and there did the sun find room enough to send a ray through the mass of foliage.

"You won't find many deer in here," Buttons remarked as they trudged along. "There's not enough for them to eat."

After the group had hiked a distance, everyone stopped to rest and take a drink from the canteens. Then they set off again.

"That line on the map shouldn't be far from here," Mr. Bobbsey said, "if my memory is correct."

"You're right, Dick," Cliff Everett agreed. "The cleared land should be right up ahead."

A short time later it seemed to the Bobbsey twins as if the forest had suddenly ended. Big trees were no longer around them. Instead, a green slope lay beyond, covered with trees only a few feet tall.

On one side of the ridge stood a tall row of trees. Bert looked up at them and remarked, "That's the seed block, isn't it, Dad?"

"Right, son. And you see how it has already reseeded the acreage which was stripped of its big trees."

Bert was eager to begin searching immediately. "The treasure might be right under our feet," the boy said, glancing about everywhere.

"Yes, but where do we start?" Freddie asked.

Mr. Bobbsey suggested that they look at the map again. As Joe Fleetwood gazed at it, he said, "I would judge that line passes two hundred yards from where we're standing."

The twins ran on ahead with Policeman Joe. Traveling now was easy, but many big stumps lay in their path. Finally they reached the area indicated on the map.

"There certainly is no circle of trees here," Joe said as he shielded his eyes from the sun and gazed about. Then he remarked sadly, "The line that the chief mentioned stretches many miles, even on your property. It will take a long, long time to cover all of it on foot."

Suddenly Bert cried out, "I know a good way to try to find the circle of trees. Couldn't we use a helicopter? We could see better from the air."

"Great idea!" Joe declared. "Why didn't we think of that before?"

"But," Mrs. Bobbsey said, "where do we get a helicopter?"

Joe Fleetwood grinned broadly and replied, "I can borrow one from the police department."

"You can?" the Bobbsey twins chorused.

"Sure. Watch." The officer switched on his walkie-talkie and contacted his superior officer.

"I'd like to borrow Kelly and the 'copter for a few hours," Joe said. He gave his position and was assured that the helicopter would be on its way in a few minutes.

The Bobbseys and their friends did not have long to wait. Fifteen minutes later the *rackety-rack* sound of the helicopter came to their ears, and the craft hovered into view over the hilltop.

Everyone waved to the pilot, who set his craft down gently on a level spot between two small hemlocks. When the rotors ceased turning, a grinning, freckle-faced, red-haired man stepped out of the 'copter.

"Hi, Joe!" he said. "Are you chasing crooks on your day off?"

Joe laughed and said they were searching for something else, then he introduced the Bobbseys and their friends.

"We're looking for a circle of trees and a big meadow," Bert explained to Pilot Kelly after telling the story about their search.

"The only possible place the meadow could have been," the pilot said, "is down this slope a bit. The land levels off, and a stream flows through it. I saw it from the air as I came over."

Mr. Bobbsey agreed and added, "That's right. It's near the edge of our property."

"Then let's search there," Nan suggested.

Pilot Kelly said that his helicopter would seat only four passengers.

Hearing this, Mrs. Bobbsey said, "Joe, why don't you take Bert and Nan up with you?"

"Good," the policeman said. "I'll leave my walkie-talkie with Mr. Bobbsey. If I find anything, I'll notify you by radio from the 'copter."

The four climbed inside the craft. The rotors whirred into action, and with a roar the 'copter lifted itself high into the air.

"There they go!" Freddie shouted. "Good luck! Good luck!"

As the 'copter rose higher, a lovely view unfolded itself beneath Bert and Nan. They could clearly see the hundred-acre tract which belonged to their father and Mr. Everett.

Policeman Joe instructed Kelly to fly along the line he had mentioned. The twins could see nothing below them but the new growth of green trees. Back and forth the pilot went, rising higher and then descending lower for a better view. Finally, as they hovered over a low, level spot, Nan cried out:

"I think I see it!"

"What?" Bert asked.

"The circle of trees—I mean, a circle of stumps. Look over this way!"

All eyes turned to the direction in which the girl pointed. Through the new foliage could be seen a rough circle of giant stumps, left when the fir trees had been cut.

Kelly spoke into his radio, "Calling Mr. Bobbsey. We think we've found the circle of stumps. Come and join us." He gave the directions and added, "We're going to land and investigate."

Their pulses throbbing with anticipation, Bert and Nan could hardly wait until the aircraft settled to the ground directly in the middle of the circle of stumps.

But before they could get out, a message came to them on the helicopter's radio. It was from Mr. Bobbsey, who sounded excited.

"We've found *Peggy!*" he told them. "And guess what, Bert and Nan! The dog Buster was tied by a chain to one of the wheels! He's all right—just hungry."

Mr. Bobbsey went on to say that the tractor had been discovered in the forest which fringed his acreage.

"How did the thief ever get it there?" Bert wanted to know.

His father replied that they had found another, newer road built right up to the edge of the cleared land.

"So there *is* something in this area that someone thinks is important," Mr. Bobbsey said. Then he added, "According to the location, you're about a mile away from us. We'll hurry to you as soon as possible."

Carrying the shovels and spades, Bert, Nan, and Joe climbed out of the 'copter and started to dig exactly in the center of the circle. Shortly afterwards they heard the shouts of their companions, who hastened to join them.

Buster, the spaniel watchdog, frolicked about his master and mistress, who were overjoyed to find their pet safe. When the spaniel saw the children digging, he gave an excited bark. Soon his front paws were working furiously, and the dirt flew back of him.

"Good old Buster," Freddie said. "He's helping us find the treasure."

Everybody dug busily for half an hour. The hole grew deeper and wider. Finally Mr. Bobbsey stopped and leaned on his shovel.

"Whew!" he said. "Nothing in sight so far. I hope this is not a wild-goose chase."

Suddenly Buster yelped. He put his nose to the freshly dug earth and sniffed.

"I think he's found something!" Nan called out.

Buster dug still deeper into the hole, and the others pitched in with their tools to help him.

Freddie, a minute later, shrieked, "The treasure!" Buster's paws had struck the top of a metal box.

Excitedly the group dug around it.

"Wow!" Bert exclaimed. "It's an enormous box!"

Kelly grinned. "I guess your search is over, folks."

"What's this made of?" Nan asked as she touched the metal casing on the box.

"Tin," Mr. Bobbsey replied. "Pure tin. If it's been here many years, that's why it hasn't rotted."

Straining and tugging, the searchers finally pulled the box free.

"What's in it? What's in it?" Flossie asked, jumping up and down in excitement.

"Yes, please open it!" Freddie begged.

Policeman Joe produced a strong knife. Working carefully, he made a slit in the tin covering of the treasure box. Then he pried the top of it loose.

Everyone gasped when the contents were revealed.

"What a surprise!" cried Freddie. "Now we're rich!"

"It's valuable all right," said Mr. Bobbsey,

Everyone gasped when the contents were revealed

"but not valuable enough for any crooks to go to the lengths Flatnose did to get it."

The box contained an amazing assortment of articles—heaps of old coins, and household utensils of all kinds; dishes, cups, and saucers; a few antiquated rifles, some ammunition, and a dozen or so beautiful old dolls.

"Look!" Flossie exclaimed, pointing to the dolls. "Aren't they just the kind you wanted, Nan?"

Nan said they were, but she wondered if the old possessions belonged to them.

"Finders keepers," Freddie spoke up.

"Is it, Dad?" Bert asked. "Or isn't this rightfully Policeman Joe's?"

Mr. Bobbsey said this certainly would be the case, if the box *had* belonged to the pioneer Wheelers from whom Joe was descended.

"Oh, I'm sure it's theirs," Nan declared. "And that this box is the meaning of the message on the cedar bark."

Mr. Everett nodded approvingly. "Sounds logical."

Policeman Joe himself smiled and turned to Nan and Flossie. "If the treasure *is* mine, would you like the dolls?" he asked.

For answer, the girls squealed in delight and bent down to pick up the lovely dolls. As they did, the sound of an airplane buzzed close overhead. Everyone looked up quickly at the sky.

"The red plane!" Bert cried out. "Do you suppose—"

The aircraft dived low, directly over their heads. Instinctively the group flattened themselves to the ground. The plane zoomed up and flew on.

Joe Fleetwood whistled. "Mighty close! That pilot dived deliberately to get a good look at us—he's no friend of ours!"

"I'll bet it's Radkin," Bert said.

"Well, he won't get away with this," Joe declared sternly.

Picking up his walkie-talkie, he radioed to headquarters, advising that they check on all local airports. "If the red plane lands, hold the pilot for questioning," Joe ordered.

Meanwhile, the Bobbseys continued to search through the old possessions. It was Mrs. Bobbsey who found a note, written on yellowed paper. Holding it gently in her hands, the twins' mother read the message hastily penned so many years before:

"We are about to be attacked by Indians, so we are burying many of our possessions here. If we survive, we can return and dig up what remains of our worldly goods. If not, God be with our children, Mary Lou and Douglas."

Everyone was silent for a moment. Nan wiped a tear from a corner of her eye. The boys and men looked on gravely.

"Those poor, unfortunate people," Mrs. Bobbsey murmured. "But, at least, Joe, this note proves that the treasure belongs to you." She handed the old paper to the officer.

"Yes, it does," said Joe, swallowing hard and turning his head away as if to hide his feelings.

Then, handling the old relics carefully, Bert and Freddie helped the men carry them to the 'copter. Just before everything was loaded, the radio lighted up. Joe quickly answered the call. After a lively conversation, he turned to the Bobbseys.

"Great news!" he said. "The man in the red plane has been captured. Just as I suspected, he landed at a small airport near by."

"Is he—?" Nan paused breathlessly.

Joe grinned. "Yes, he's your Mr. Radkin, all right. He's confessed that he's the one who called himself 'the boss.' The police have a full confession from him."

Policeman Joe went on to say that Radkin had once heard from a former resident of Silver Creek that there was a great treasure on the Bobbsey-Everett property. He had figured that it was either gold or oil. He determined to get hold of the land by any means whatever. The photo of the cedar bark showing the circle of thirteen dots had been found in his wallet.

"I'll see that my cousin, Mr. Wheeler, gets back his picture, as well as his share of the treasure," added the officer.

"Oh boy," said Bert, chuckling, "was Mr. Radkin ever fooled!"

"Yes." Flossie giggled. "What would he have done with those dolls?"

"Speaking of dolls," Joe went on, "Radkin also admitted that he was the one who stole your toys at Lakeport. He did it to throw suspicion on someone named Danny, after the boy refused to work for him any longer."

"Well, good for Danny!" said Bert. "Maybe he's not such a bad guy after all!"

"Oh, I don't know," Freddie spoke up skeptically. "He likes to play tricks on us too much."

"What about Mr. Flatnose?" Nan asked Joe. "Has he confessed yet?"

The policeman said that Radkin had confessed for him. Flatnose, whose real name was Tatum, had been ordered by Radkin to steal Buster and the tractor, and to start the fire in the woods. Also, it was Flatnose who had unsuccessfully tried to take Mr. Everett's chainsaw.

"And Mr. Berryman," the officer went on, "was working for Radkin, too. He's a pilot, and he was on the plane when Radkin was caught."

The Bobbseys learned, too, that it was Radkin who had damaged the lumber trucks in Lakeport. He had put Mr. Taylor up to trying to buy Mr. Bobbsey's share in the Silver Creek property.

"And did that awful Mr. Radkin make Mr. Taylor send Dad the telegram about the lumber-yard fire?" Nan asked.

"Right you are," said Policeman Joe.

"Hurray!" Freddie cried, jumping up and down. "Now all the mysteries have been solved!"

"All but one," said Buttons. "What about my stolen shirt?"

"Oh," Flossie piped up. "We found the rest of it by the tractor. Buster was lying on it." She looked at the logger in surprise. "Do you want it back?"

Buttons grinned broadly. "No. You see, all I care about are the buttons. I take three of them off each shirt to avoid bad luck. But for good luck, I keep them." Then he winked. "I guess the stolen shirt minus the buttons brought all of us luck, at that."

"It sure did," Bert agreed, and Freddie cried out, "Three cheers for our forest adventure!"